sew zoey

A TANGLED THREAD

written by
Chloe Taylor

illustrated by
Nancy Zhang

Simon Spotlight

New York   London   Toronto   Sydney   New Delhi

SIMON SPOTLIGHT
An imprint of Simon & Schuster Children's Publishing Division
1230 Avenue of the Americas, New York, New York 10020
Copyright © 2014 by Simon & Schuster, Inc.
All rights reserved, including the right of reproduction in whole or
in part in any form.
SIMON SPOTLIGHT and colophon are registered trademarks of
Simon & Schuster, Inc.
Text by Caroline Hickey
Designed by Laura Roode
For information about special discounts for bulk purchases, please contact
Simon & Schuster Special Sales at 1-866-506-1949 or
business@simonandschuster.com.
Manufactured in the United States of America 0214 OFF
First Edition 10 9 8 7 6 5 4 3 2 1
ISBN 978-1-4814-0443-3 (pb)
ISBN 978-1-4814-0444-0 (hc)
ISBN 978-1-4814-0445-7 (eBook)
Library of Congress Catalog Card Number 2013943454

-------- CHAPTER 1 --------

Brand-New News!!!

The great thing about fashion is that there's always something NEW happening, right? Well, my life's like that too. I earned enough money from my Doggie Duds campaign to do some serious shopping for brand-new fabric, including the really pricey kind that I usually drool over from afar. I can't WAIT to get started on some new projects!

And speaking of new projects—drumroll, please—I'm also superthrilled to announce my next venture! Actually, it's a team thing. I'm going to be launching a collaboration Etsy store with another young designer, Allie Lovallo (with our parents monitoring, of course). Some of you might know her from our feature together on TresChic.com, or from her blog, Always Allie Accessories. The store will be called Accessories from A to Z, and—you guessed it!—we're going to be focusing on accessories! It's a pop-up shop that will be online for a limited time only, so get 'em while they're hot!

When we came up with the idea, I was going to sew clothes and she was going to make accessories, and we were going to call it Fashion from A to Z. The thing is, sizing clothes is complicated, while accessories are usually one-size-fits-most. So we decided to have an accessories store with some Allie stuff (Allie's the *A*) and some Zoey stuff (I'm the *Z*). It's going to be *A* for "awesome." As you can see from my sketch of some of the things I'm offering, I've already been hard at work. But I want to hear from you, readers. Let me know what else you'd like to see in our store!

We're launching the site as soon as we can, so this weekend I'll be doing all the last-minute work to get it ready. Tonight, though, I have a very important movie date— with two of my best friends! TGIF!

"More chocolate chips," Priti Holbrooke insisted. "Really, we need *more*."

Zoey Webber and Libby Flynn eyed each other skeptically, but then Zoey shrugged and went ahead and shook the entire bag of chocolate chips into the bowl. Priti grabbed a wooden spoon to fold them into the batter.

It was Friday night, and the three friends were at Libby's house, baking cookies and watching a movie, but they were barely paying attention to the screen. There was just too much to talk about! And too many chocolate chips to eat.

"We're going to have to rename these cookies chocolate *chocolate*-chip cookies," Libby said, laughing. "I've never used *two* whole bags of chips before!"

Priti smiled confidently as she folded melted chocolate into the batter. It went from a light tan color, to chocolate striped, to a deep chocolate brown. "My sisters and I *always* make them this way. Trust me."

Zoey spread out cookie sheets on the counter, and the three girls began dropping balls of dough onto them. As their hands moved back and forth, Zoey noticed that everyone was wearing their friendship bracelets. They had made the bracelets with a pattern using four different colors of metallic beads to represent each of the four best friends. There was rose gold for Priti, silver for Zoey, copper for Libby, and classic gold for their fourth BFF, Kate Mackey, who was at soccer practice that night. Kate was Zoey's oldest friend in the world, and Zoey couldn't help feeling like there was something missing without her there.

"Kate would love these," Libby said.

"Yeah, she would," Zoey agreed. "When we were little we called her the Cookie Monster. Too bad she couldn't be here."

"Well, state championships are in a few weeks,"

Priti said. "And when it's over—and she scores the winning goal—she'll have more time to hang out! And eat cookies."

Zoey nodded. "True."

"You guys!" Priti shouted suddenly. Her hand flew to her mouth. "I can't believe I forgot to tell you!"

"Tell us what?" Libby asked. She slid the loaded cookie sheets into the oven, set the timer, and turned back toward Priti in one graceful move.

"I'm going to India!" Priti squealed. "Finally. For real."

"*What?* When?" Libby and Zoey both shouted.

Priti's eyes glowed. "My cousin is getting married in a few weeks, and we haven't seen most of our family in forever since they live all over the world. So all the relatives—from England, Canada, everywhere—are traveling to India for the wedding! It's going to be *huge*. Plus we're going to Delhi and the Taj Mahal."

Immediately, Zoey began picturing a big Indian wedding, with beautiful music and colors and food. "Oh, Priti, that sounds so cool!"

"I haven't been to a wedding since I was a flower girl in my uncle's wedding," Libby said. "You're going to have so much fun!"

"I know!" Priti said gleefully. "It'll be my first big traditional Indian wedding. My mom said the groom rides in on a white horse, and the bride and groom exchange garlands to show they accept each other as spouses. The celebration goes on for days. And everyone wears the most *amaaaaazing* saris. . . ."

Priti dug around in her bag to pull out her phone. She typed in a search term and held out the phone so Zoey and Libby could see as she scrolled through the pictures of Indian saris. Despite the distracting smell of cookies baking in the oven, Zoey's mind immediately went into fashion overdrive.

"Oh my gosh, Priti!" she said, grabbing the phone so she could get a better look. "These *are* amazing! Look at the colors!"

Zoey kept shuffling through the pictures, completely entranced by the bright, jewel-tone colors; metallic embellishments; and sumptuousness of the fabrics. Her mind was already buzzing with ideas. How had she never noticed before that saris were the most beautiful dresses on Earth?

"They look complicated to put on," Libby said, studying one picture over Zoey's shoulder. "Are they one piece?"

"Some are, some aren't," Priti explained. "Some have a little top that's separate, and some just fold over one shoulder. It's, like, nine different steps to wrap one properly. My mom knows how, and my sisters, but I don't. There's a lot of tucking and pleating, and it takes a lot of patience!"

Zoey was barely listening. Already an idea was forming in her mind of how *she'd* design a sari, using one of those beautiful, beautiful fabrics, but making the style a bit more contemporary.

"My mom would never let me wear one like *that*," Libby said, pointing. All the girls looked at one picture, which showed a woman in a sari with a bit of midriff showing on the side. "She'd say it's too *risqué*."

Priti laughed. "Things are different in India. My *grandmother* wears a sari like that! It looks great, actually."

They all laughed before the ding of the kitchen timer interrupted them. Libby grabbed an oven mitt to take the cookies out to cool.

"Well, your grandmother may wear one," Libby said, "but my mom would probably make me put a cardigan over it!"

The girls giggled again, and Zoey noticed Libby's dog, Chester, coming into the kitchen. He was wearing the Doggie Duds clothes she'd made for him, an outfit with a little tie sewn on it, and he looked very spiffy. His nose was twitching fiercely, and he tried to stand up on his back legs to see where the delicious smell was coming from.

"He's wearing his outfit!" Zoey said, pleased. There was nothing more flattering to a designer than seeing someone wearing the clothes she'd made for them.

Libby nodded. "He wears it all the time. My mom says when she takes him to the dog park, people stop her constantly to say how cute it is."

Zoey blushed. She still wasn't used to compliments about her work, even though she got them pretty often now. "Thanks! I really had fun with the Doggie Duds campaign—but I'm glad it's over! I'm ready for something new to sink my teeth into. Starting with that cookie."

As Zoey reached for a hot cookie, Libby playfully rapped Zoey's fingers with a plastic spatula. "Not yet!" she said. "They're really hot."

"You want something new?" Priti asked Zoey, clutching her arm. "I have the perfect idea!"

"What?" asked Libby.

"What?" echoed Zoey.

"I need something to wear for my cousin's wedding! And who could design a better sari than you, Zoey! Right? Would you?"

Zoey didn't have to think for long. Design a modern-day sari for one of her best friends to wear to a gorgeous wedding in India? It was a fashion designer's dream come true!

"Yes!" Zoey yelled. "I'd love to! I've already got a million ideas. The hard part will be choosing one. We could do so many different things. . . ."

Libby clapped her hands. "Yay! It's settled. That'll be so great!"

Priti frowned suddenly. "Well, mostly settled. I

just want to *double-check* with my mom that it'll be okay. Since it's a traditional ceremony and all. I'm sure it'll be fine, but I'll ask her right away. Okay?"

"Okay!" Zoey agreed. The two girls hugged, and Libby presented them with a plate piled high with cookies.

"Time to eat!" she declared.

They moved over to the couch where the movie was still playing. They each dug themselves into a comfortable nook on the big sectional and munched on cookies. Priti was right—the cookies were awesome.

"Priti, these are the *best* cookies in the entire world! Have you ever thought about starting a baking blog to go with your mom's cooking blog? You could call it KarmaKid instead of KarmaMama!" Zoey suggested as she took her third cookie in three minutes.

"Well, I do know a lot about chocolate chips," Priti said. "Mostly that they're really yummy. But I think one cooking blogger in the family is enough."

"Actually, speaking of blogs," Zoey began, "Allie

and I are doing the final work for our Etsy store tomorrow, before it launches. Would you guys mind taking a look at the page? Dad helped me, but I want to make sure it's just right, you know?"

"Would I *mind*?" Priti joked after rushing to swallow a bite of cookie. "I'd love to!"

"I'll help too!" Libby said. "And would you let me know when the shop is up and running? I want to tell my aunt about it."

Zoey hesitated a moment. Libby's aunt was a buyer for one of the biggest and best department stores in the country—H. Cashin's. In the past, Libby had been reluctant to involve her aunt in Zoey's fashion-related endeavors, in case it seemed like Zoey was using her for her aunt's connections. While they had worked it out, Zoey didn't want there to be any awkwardness.

"I will," Zoey said cautiously, "but only tell her if you want to. Okay? Don't feel like you have to."

Libby nodded. "I know. I feel much better about . . . all that . . . since the sewing contest thing. She was so impressed with you, she told me *specifically* to let her know whenever you had news. I even told her about your Doggie Duds campaign!"

"Aw, thanks, Libby." Zoey blushed again. She felt like the luckiest girl in the world sometimes, having friends as nice as Priti and Libby and Kate. And now on top of everything, she was going to design a sari that would travel to India!

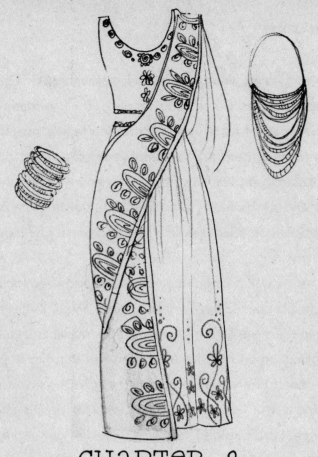

CHAPTER 2

Not Sari at All!

I am in love. LOVE. No, really, I am! And I'm not ashamed of it. But it's not with a person—I'm in love with SARIS! You know, those beautiful dresses that Indian women wear? Apparently, the word "sari" means "strip of cloth" (I looked it up!), and they come in an amazing rainbow of shiny jewel tones with gold or silver thread accents. But the coolest part, I think, is that there are so many ways to wear them. It seems like most wear a matching fitted top and wrap the long piece of sari fabric around their waist to make a skirt . . . then throw the end of the fabric over their shoulder in a dramatic swoop. I uploaded a sketch of a traditional one here to show you.

Anyway, I'm completely obsessed and keep looking them up online. Why would anyone EVER wear jeans when there are saris in the world? Seriously! I'm already working on an idea for a modern sari that I'm hoping my friend Priti will get to wear to her cousin's wedding in India in a few weeks. Stay tuned for details and a sketch. I can't upload it now because I'm getting ready to launch Accessories from A to Z! I loved the ideas you sent in for accessories to add—I think I'm going to add the fabric necklaces and bracelets!

Zoey and Allie sat in Zoey's living room, surrounded by an enormous mess. There were stacks of accessories everywhere, along with notes about each product, Zoey's laptop, a few bottles of water, and two bags of gummy bears that the girls were snacking on as they tried to organize everything. Zoey had been a little nervous about Allie coming over to help, since she didn't really know her *that* well. Plus, Allie was sixteen and in high school. But when Allie had shown up holding two bags of gummy bears—wearing a black zebra-striped tee, fuchsia jean shorts, and handmade bangle bracelets—Zoey felt certain the day would go smoothly.

The week before, Allie had explained to Zoey how to take well-lit pictures of each item so that customers looking at the pictures online could get a really clear idea of what they were buying. Zoey's older brother, Marcus, had helped Zoey take the pictures, since he liked fooling around with photo and video editing.

Today, Allie and Zoey decided to start by editing the descriptions of each item Zoey had already uploaded to the site's content management system. Zoey and Allie huddled around Zoey's laptop on the coffee table.

"So the most important thing to remember when

you're writing your descriptions," Allie was saying, "is to make sure to include dimensions, materials, special features, and things like that. These already look good, but I think we can make them more fun."

Zoey nodded, taking mental notes as Allie reviewed the descriptions.

"On my Always Allie store page, I've noticed it helps to mention something I think the accessory would go particularly well with, to help the customer imagine how and where they might wear it," Allie said. "For example, for this clutch we could say 'This vibrant clutch would spice up a black shift dress or a pair of jeans.' Sound okay?"

"Sounds great," Zoey said. "Wow, you really know your stuff."

"Well, thanks," Allie said. "But I've had a *little* more practice than you."

The girls went through the rest of the descriptions together and tried to make each one more customer-focused.

Allie saved the changes to the site, then flopped back onto the sofa to fish around in the bag of gummies for another handful. For a moment, she looked deep in thought, slowly chewing one gummy at a time.

"You know, I can't believe we're really doing this!" Allie said. "I mean, working together, like real business partners."

"Definitely!" Zoey giggled. "Working together" sounded so grown-up, like she was an adult with an office job and coworkers. But she and Allie *were* working together, and Zoey felt very lucky. Allie seemed pretty grown up. She was a junior and planned to attend Parsons The New School for Design in New York City after she graduated.

"Is there anything else I should be doing to get ready for the launch?" Zoey asked.

"*Wellll*, I usually keep a stack of packing materials and labels handy, so I can send off orders as soon as I get them," Allie said. "Because if you let them pile up, you'll get overwhelmed, and your inventory count can get messed up. And customers appreciate it when their orders arrive quickly."

Zoey was already a little overwhelmed.

"Hey, Zoey, what's all this stuff—" Marcus stopped midsentence as he walked into the living room, which was covered with headbands, purses, necklaces, and envelopes. He was carrying his drumsticks, which he was playing in the air as he walked in. "Oh, whoops." The drumsticks froze as he noticed Allie on the couch. "Hey. I'm . . . um . . . Marcus," he said.

"This is Allie," said Zoey. "You know, my Etsy store partner." Zoey giggled again as she said the word "partner." All those business-y words seemed way too grown-up. "Allie, this is my brother."

Allie didn't giggle. But her cheeks turned slightly red as she said hello to Marcus.

"You guys look, uh, busy," he said, gesturing at all the products. "Are you going to be ready for your launch?"

Allie nodded, running one hand through her long mane of brown curls to smooth it. "We'll be ready tomorrow," she said, smiling. "I think." Suddenly, she turned to Zoey. "That reminds me," she said excitedly. "I e-mailed TresChic.com to tell them about the launch of Accessories from A to Z, and I asked them to link to it at the end of their feature about us and the other young designers. They were game, so now anyone who reads the article will be directed right to our online store!"

"Wow!" Zoey squealed. She never would have thought of that. "What a great idea!"

"Nice work," Marcus said, looking impressed. He was still standing at the edge of the mess, holding his drumsticks in the air. "You guys might really sell some stuff. Do you need any help?"

"No, thanks," Zoey said quickly, anxious for her and Allie to get back to work. They still had a lot to do. "But you can take some gummy bears if you want."

Marcus stepped forward, nearly tripping over some scarves, and took a handful of gummies. Zoey noticed that his cheeks were bright red. He stepped back and stood awkwardly for a second before giving the girls a sort of half wave and heading out of the room.

Zoey and Allie worked hard for the next two hours, checking the spelling of the text on the site, getting Zoey's dad's final approval to launch, and then organizing all of Zoey's merchandise and packing materials in the dining room so that when orders started coming in, she'd be ready. When the living room was finally cleaned up, Allie and Zoey sat on the couch, the laptop resting on Zoey's lap.

"Are we ready?" Allie asked. "Launch time?"

"Yes! Time to lift off!" Zoey replied. Her knees jiggled the laptop. She couldn't believe how excited she was. The Doggie Duds campaign on Myfundmaker had been great, but those outfits had been given as gifts in return for people's donations to her campaign. This would be her first time really trying to *sell* her designs. Would it work? Would anyone *buy* anything?

"Okay, let's launch!" said Allie. "Go ahead—you do the honors."

Zoey moved the mouse so it was positioned over the Make it Live button. Her heart was thumping in her chest. Somehow, pressing that button felt like the beginning of something very big. No longer would she just be blogging and posting sketches and making things for herself and friends. She would be selling her work alongside other designers.

It was a big step.

Zoey took a deep breath and clicked the mouse.

A few seconds later, Accessories from A to Z popped up in the browser, live for the whole world to see.

"Mission accomplished!" cried Allie. "We did it!"

She gave Zoey a big hug. Zoey had already started to think of her as a real friend, and she hoped that the accessories store would be just the first of many ventures together!

"Did I hear some happy shouting?" asked Zoey's father, poking his head in the doorway. He peeked into the dining room at the tidy piles of materials and accessories. "Is it official?"

Zoey was beaming. "Yep! We launched it, Dad. It's live! Our site is live."

Mr. Webber strode in and gave Zoey a huge hug. "Way to go, Zo! I'm really proud of you." He reached over and patted Allie's shoulder. "And you too, Allie. I'd love to take you girls out to celebrate, but I've got to get to a game, and I won't be back for a few hours."

Zoey's dad was a sports therapist and worked for the local university, monitoring the health of the athletes. He attended most games, and Zoey sometimes went with him, even though she could barely tell a kickoff from a field goal.

Out of nowhere, Marcus appeared in the doorway. "You know, Dad, I could take Zoey and Allie out for ice cream," he offered. Marcus had gotten his license recently, and he had a new car, so he was happy to find excuses to drive places. He had been saving up money from his life-guarding gig to buy a car when their dad surprised him with a gently used (but new-to-Marcus) sedan. Their dad liked it because it was safe, and Marcus liked it because it had wheels.

Zoey lit up. "Really, Marcus? Thanks! Allie, do you want to?"

Allie nodded, looking pleased. "Sure, that sounds fun. If you don't mind, that is . . . ," she mumbled in Marcus's direction.

"No problem," Marcus said. He cleared his throat. "I could even drive Allie home afterward. You know, if she needs a ride."

Allie nodded. "Um, yeah, sure! Thanks. I'll text my mom and let her know she doesn't need to come get me."

Zoey dashed off a text message too—to let her

friends know the Etsy shop was officially open for business. In seconds, her phone was buzzing with incoming texts congratulating her and Allie.

Zoey's dad left for the game, and Marcus, Allie, and Zoey piled into Marcus's car and headed to Zoey's favorite ice-cream parlor.

At the counter, Zoey said hello to the owner, Mrs. Simms, who'd known Zoey since she was little.

"Hello, Zoey and Marcus!" Mrs. Simms said. "Great to see you. We've got two special flavors today—Rainbow Delight and Marshmallow Mint."

Zoey looked through all the flavors, and after careful consideration, ordered a double-scoop cone of mint chocolate chip and Rainbow Delight. She loved mixing different flavors together, just as she loved mixing different fabrics together. It made everything more interesting.

"This flavor combo should be just right for you," said Mrs. Simms, handing Zoey the cone. "And how about for your friend?"

"This is Allie," said Zoey.

Allie and Mrs. Simms said hello to each other,

and Allie said she was ready to order.

"I think I'll have a single scoop of Marshmallow Mint," Allie declared. Then, with a glance at Zoey's huge cone, changed her mind. "Well, since we're celebrating, make it a double."

"Celebrating?" said Mrs. Simms. "What are you celebrating, Zoey?"

Zoey was so distracted by the delicious ice cream, she'd nearly forgotten. She said, "Oh right! Yes, we are. Allie and I just launched an accessories site together on Etsy.com!"

Mrs. Simms applauded. "Way to go, Zoey! I'll check it out tonight! In the meantime, these cones are on the house." She winked at the girls and Marcus.

"Wow! Thank you, Mrs. Simms!" Zoey couldn't believe how nice and supportive everyone was being. Her brother had taken her out for ice cream, and now the ice cream was free! It was an important day for sure. "How about I make you a special fabric headband using the colors of the ice-cream parlor logo as a thank-you?" she suggested.

Mrs. Simms nodded, looking pleased. "That

sounds excellent. Then I can tell all my customers where to buy their own when they compliment me on it! Deal?"

"Deal!" Zoey replied. Nearly giddy with excitement, she followed Marcus and Allie to a high table by the window.

When they were seated, the three of them raised their cones and clinked them, like they were toasting with glasses. Marcus said, "Congratulations, Zoey and Allie!"

Zoey was really touched by how proud Marcus seemed to be. He'd always encouraged her interest in fashion, though she was pretty sure some of that had to do with the fact that their mother had loved fashion and sewing clothes too. And maybe it made Marcus feel like their mother, who had died when Zoey was very, very young, wasn't totally gone.

Zoey sewed on her mom's old sewing machine and used a lot of her mother's old clothes for inspiration, and even to mix in with her own wardrobe. Sewing was a way to stay connected to the mom she hadn't had much of a chance to get to know. Her father would tell her every now and then how much she reminded him of her mother, and Zoey loved to hear it, even if it made her a little sad.

Zoey, Marcus, and Allie were enjoying their huge, double scoop cones when suddenly they heard a cell phone buzzing.

"It's mine, I think," said Zoey, assuming it was a text from Priti or Kate.

"Nope, I think it's me," said Allie.

They both reached for their phones and shrieked at the exact same time.

"What is it?" asked Marcus, sounding alarmed. "What happened?"

"I made my first sale!" each girl shouted at the same time. Then they looked up at each other. "You *did*?"

Allie clicked through the automated e-mail alert from Etsy to read the name of the buyer. "Hmm, it's someone named . . . *Lulu*. Cool name."

Immediately, Zoey and Marcus burst out laughing. Zoey checked her e-mail, and, of course, her order was from Lulu as well.

"Why are you laughing?" Allie asked.

"Lulu is our aunt," Marcus explained. "And one

of Zoey's biggest fans."

"I bet she's been sitting at her computer all day hitting refresh and waiting for the site to go live so she could order something from each of us," Zoey said.

"For sure," Marcus agreed.

Allie shrugged. "An order's an order!" she said, delighted. "Even if it's from a relative. I'll get it to her right away."

Zoey was excited too, but part of her wondered if she would sell anything to anyone other than Mrs. Simms, her aunt Lulu, and her closest friends. Maybe the Etsy store would be for relatives only.

Even if it is, she told herself, *it's still fun making the accessories. And I can always give them to friends later on.*

Zoey decided that now was not the time to worry about the Etsy store, not when she had a huge ice-cream cone in front of her. She went back to enjoying her double scoop as Marcus and Allie began talking about friends they had in common, even though they went to different high schools.

A huge drip from Zoey's cone hit the table. As

she hurried to lick up any other drips, she couldn't help noticing how slowly and neatly Marcus was eating. Usually, he scarfed down an ice-cream cone like a starving man. He was even wiping his mouth with a napkin occasionally, something she'd seen him do only at special events and holiday dinners.

Allie was eating neatly too, like her cone was fragile and precious. But she also had chewed her gummy bears slowly. Zoey had noticed that while she was practically inhaling them, herself.

Maybe you have to be really proper when you're in high school, thought Zoey. *If so, I'm glad I'm still in middle school and can eat my ice cream any way I want!*

-------- CHAPTER 3 --------

Accessories Accomplished!

Guess what, guess what? The Accessories from A to Z site is now live! I'm so excited!!! Not only that, I've already gotten my very first order for a clutch purse. (Sure, it's from a member of my own family, but it still counts! Right?) Allie and I worked soooooo hard over the weekend getting it ready to launch, and we ended up celebrating with some extremely delicious ice cream. From now on, I plan to celebrate everything with a double scoop of mint chocolate chip and Rainbow Delight! Feel free to try this at home.

In other news, I've been working hard on my design for my friend Priti's modern sari. I've added some ruffles to the bottom (because that's SEW Priti) and a dramatic swoop of fabric over the shoulder. That's going to be the tricky part when sewing it. . . . I've got to make sure it'll stay put while she's dancing! I've never worked with a style of dress that wraps like this, so it's probably going to take me a few tries to get it right. All I need now is the okay from Priti and her mom (and some good sewing mojo!), and I can start my first sari!

When I finish, I plan to celebrate with—you guessed it—ICE CREAM! Two scoops!

At school on Monday, Zoey sat at her regular table in the cafeteria with her friends, Kate, Priti, and Libby. Being at school was a welcome distraction from the fact that Zoey hadn't gotten another Etsy order since her aunt's order the other day. Zoey had told herself not to get her hopes up about the site, but she couldn't help it. She wanted people to buy her accessories! She'd spent the evening checking her phone every ten minutes for Etsy e-mails. Being at school in the busy, loud lunchroom was a kind of escape from wondering.

"Zoey," said Priti, grabbing Zoey's arm. "I have news! I talked to my mom this morning and explained that I wanted you to make a modern sari for me to wear at the wedding, and she said *yes*!"

Libby and Kate both clapped, and Zoey dropped her sandwich. She was that excited. "So I get to make the sari? And you're going to wear it in India?"

Priti nodded happily. "Yes! She was checking her e-mail, so, well, she was a little distracted. But she said yes! Hooray!"

Zoey immediately began digging in her backpack for her sketchbook. She pulled it out and flipped to the page with the sketch she'd done of the sari. "This is what I was thinking . . . ," she said, showing it to all the girls. "See the ruffles here?"

The girls oohed and ahhed over Zoey's design.

"I love the ruffles," said Priti, "and I love the whole design! I saw it on your blog this morning!"

"Me too," said Kate. "I've started to check your blog before I leave for school each morning so I know what's going on with you! I've missed so much with all my soccer practices."

Zoey giggled. "Thanks, Kate. Don't worry—you get a pass until the season's over."

Libby, who was holding the sketchbook, nodded her head admiringly. "I don't know how you come up with this stuff, Zoey! It's soooo beautiful. Priti, can I come to the wedding too?"

The girls laughed, and Libby handed the sketchbook back to Zoey.

"Speaking of beautiful dresses," said Kate, pulling a catalog from her backpack and opening it to a dog-eared page on the table in front of them. "What do you guys think of this dress? I've got the big spaghetti dinner for my soccer team soon, and I need something to wear. My mom is going to order this one if I don't choose something else."

Zoey studied the picture. The dress was a pastel floral print, with long sleeves, a collar, and a sash.

It looked like something Kate would have liked when she was a little girl, not like twelve-year-old Kate at all.

Zoey bit her lip, unsure how to reply. She knew Kate could look really amazing in something more modern, but she didn't want to hurt Kate's feelings by telling her she didn't think the dress was right for her.

Out of nowhere, Ivy Wallace, Shannon Chang, and Bree Sharpe, their school's notorious trio of girls who were known for always saying the meanest thing possible in any situation, appeared. Zoey wondered if they spent the lunch hour wandering around the cafeteria, listening to other people's conversations so they could offer their two cents. They were always in the right place at the right time—which was the wrong time for anyone who wasn't in their group.

They stopped behind Zoey, and Ivy bent over her shoulder to study the catalog picture. Zoey resisted the urge to swat Ivy away like the pesky fly she was.

"Pretty dress, Kate," Ivy said with a sneer. "I assume you'll be riding your tricycle to the soccer dinner? Will your mommy give you a lollipop if you behave?"

Zoey watched as Kate's eyebrows pulled together, her face growing redder by the second. It made Zoey's stomach turn.

Then Bree chimed in. "I have a dress *exactly* like this, Kate—but it's boxed up in the attic with all the other clothes I wore in *kindergarten*!"

She and Ivy burst into laughter. Only Shannon, her face as red as Kate's, stayed quiet. Shannon had been a good friend of Zoey's in elementary school, before she'd started hanging out with Ivy. Ivy was a bad influence on everyone around her. *She's poison ivy, really,* thought Zoey.

"Buzz off, girls," said Priti. "You're obviously over your fashion heads. You wouldn't know a great-looking, classic design if it bit you in the ankle."

Zoey joined Priti in glaring at the three girls until they moved on to another table.

Zoey looked at Kate, worried she'd been wounded. "I'm so sorry they said that, Kate! Don't worry—the dress will look great."

To everyone's surprise, Kate burst out laughing. "Hahahahaha! I know this dress is hideous. That's why I'm showing it to you! My mom wants to get it for me, but I want *you* to design me something else!"

Zoey was surprised but happy to hear those words come out of Kate's mouth. Kate had never asked Zoey to make her clothes before, and she was a terrific muse! Athletic and tan, there were a million things that would look great on Kate. The possibilities were endless!

"Oooh, I can't wait! Really? Oh my gosh! Did you ask your mom if I could?" Zoey asked.

Kate shrugged. "Well, sort of. She said as long as it's *appropriate*, she'll be happy. And I say as long as I don't look like my grandmother's floral wallpaper, *I'll* be happy!"

The girls all cheered and put their hands in the middle of the table together, clinking their bracelets, Ivy's and Bree's nasty comments already forgotten.

"Sounds like I've got a lot of sewing to do," said Zoey. "I'd better get started right away."

"I've got a bag of sari fabric I can bring over," Priti offered helpfully. "It's in my mom's closet."

"And I can pay for my fabric," said Kate. "I've got allowance saved up—"

"No way," Zoey cut in. "I've got my Doggie Duds money. And I've been dying to make you something. This one's on me."

"Thanks, Zo," said Kate softly, and the two girls shared a look of understanding that only girls who had been good friends for many years could share.

Lunch dissolved into discussions of what would look best on Kate, what kind of dress went with spaghetti, and how well Priti had told off Ivy. Zoey was itching to start sketching so she could get the ideas down on paper. She had to make the best dress ever for Kate!

Between classes, Zoey called her aunt and asked her to pick her up after school. She needed a ride to A Stitch in Time to get fabric for Kate's dress. Lulu had agreed on the spot and was waiting out front when the final bell rang.

Zoey's aunt Lulu was an interior decorator

with her own business, so not only was she often available at odd times to run errands with Zoey or offer advice, she also knew her way around a fabric store. Zoey had spent many happy afternoons at her aunt's house just looking through the mountains of fabric swatches she kept on hand for her clients.

When Zoey saw Lulu's car, she hopped in and started talking a mile a minute. On the way to the store, Zoey filled her aunt in on the two new projects she was beginning—making a sari for Priti and a dress for Kate. Aunt Lulu loved to hear about Zoey's sewing and read her blog religiously.

"I've already seen the sari sketch on your blog," she told Zoey. "I think it'll look marvelous. I'm so glad Priti has fabric for you though—those sari fabrics can be pricey."

"Well, I have my Doggie Duds money," Zoey said. She glanced in the backseat, where Lulu's dog, Buttons, sat dressed in her Doggie Duds cape. "It's nice to see my doggie clients are still happy with their outfits!"

"Buttons is a very satisfied customer," Lulu said. They pulled into the parking lot of the fabric store, got out of the car, and hooked Buttons's leash to her collar, so they could bring her inside. Jan, the store owner, loved dogs, as long as they didn't make messes in the store.

"And speaking of satisfied customers," said Lulu, as they headed into the store. "I can't tell you how much I love this purse!" Zoey had given the purse to her aunt the day before. Aunt Lulu waved it over her head, as if there was an imaginary crowd around them, watching. "Hey, everyone, my amazing niece made this clutch!"

Buttons barked and Zoey laughed and pulled her aunt's arm down. There was nothing like going fabric shopping with your number-one fan.

Inside the fabric store, Zoey inhaled deeply. She loved the scent of the fabrics. They smelled fresh and new and full of possibilities. Normally, Zoey kept to one end of the store where the better bargains were found, but today she decided to explore the pricier section, where the patterns and textures made her drool.

Jan, who often made extra time to help Zoey with fabric selections and sewing problems, made a beeline toward them.

"Welcome, Zoey and Lulu . . . and Buttons! What can I help you with today?"

Jan was wearing two scarves, one a green print and one a blue, twisted together around her waist as a belt. Zoey loved it and decided she would try that herself.

Zoey explained about the soccer dinner for her friend Kate and that Kate was someone who usually didn't wear particularly girly clothes.

"Well," said Jan, "since you've got a little extra fabric money today, I'd try some of these higher-quality knits here. They're stretchy, practical, and extremely soft, which sounds like something your friend would be comfortable in."

Zoey began flipping through the fabrics on the rack and immediately fell in love with one of the knits that had a swirly print on it. It reminded her a bit of spaghetti, but in a fashion-y way. It was totally gorgeous! She'd never used a fabric quite that stretchy for clothing before, only for accessories, but something about it spoke to her, and she knew she wanted it for Kate's dress.

Lulu and Jan completely agreed with the fabric choice, and with business out of the way, Zoey was free to spend time just browsing all the beautiful things at the store. Jan even brought out some doggie treats and a bowl of water for Buttons. It was a perfect way to end the day.

At home that night, Zoey took out the fabric she'd purchased for Kate's dress and laid it out as inspiration. Then she began working in earnest on a sketch. Kate was lucky to have a figure that would look good in pretty much anything, but Zoey wanted to do more than just make Kate look good. She wanted to design a dress that Kate would love! Kate had dutifully worn things her mom had picked out for her for years, things she didn't really like, and now was her chance to wear something more *her*.

Zoey's phone buzzed, and she hastily grabbed it to see who it was. It was another e-mail from Etsy! She'd made another sale!

Relief flowed through her as she clicked through the e-mail alert and saw the name of the buyer.

She didn't recognize it. A stranger had found her accessories site and bought something. A stranger had liked one of her designs! Now she had to plan to get the order out as quickly as possible, since she had a lot of work to do designing for her friends. She turned back to her sketches for Kate, feeling like maybe, just maybe, she'd bitten off a little more than she could chew by offering to design and sew two dresses in less than two weeks *and* manage her new Etsy store. *What have I gotten myself into?* Zoey thought.

She took a deep breath and thought back to the advice she had given to Priti not so long ago, when Priti was overwhelmed. Zoey had said to take it one stitch at a time, and now she decided to do just that. Since the mail wouldn't go out until the next day, anyway, she decided to package the order later and focus on Kate's dress.

Besides, Zoey thought, *Dad always says that there's busy, and there's* good *busy. And this is definitely* good *busy!*

Surveying her sketches critically, Zoey decided Kate really looked best in more simple designs and would probably be most *comfortable* in something basic as well, so the best way to go for her would be to make a dress with a basic T-shirt–like top and use the beautiful swirly knit fabric to make an attached tulip skirt. The bit of poof in the skirt would be girly, but not too girly, for sporty Kate. And her mom would like it because tulip skirts were feminine and fun.

Zoey added some finishing touches to the sketch, certain she'd found the right balance for Kate, and then climbed into bed to do her homework.

If only my homework were designing clothes! Zoey thought. *I wouldn't mind doing it at all. . . . In fact, I'd probably turn in extra credit every week!*

CHAPTER 4

Spaghetti, Anyone?

As if things weren't interesting enough around here making a sari for my friend Priti, now I'm also designing a dress for my wonderful friend Kate to wear to her soccer team's end-of-season celebration! It's a spaghetti dinner, and I found this amazing knit fabric with a swirly pattern on it that reminds me of spaghetti. Do you like the sketch for her dress? Only the skirt part will be in the swirly fabric, and the top will be T-shirty and sporty, just like Kate. I think it's even girly enough to make her mom happy!

I've had a few sales come through Etsy, so I wanted to say thank you to my readers for their support! I hope everyone loves their accessories as much as I love the AMAAAAAAZING bag of sari fabrics Priti dropped off earlier for me to use. I opened the bag, and so much color spilled out, it was like being inside a giant bag of Skittles candies. I'm playing with them now, wrapping them around myself to see how constructing this sari will work. I'm even considering taking two fabrics and twisting or sewing them together to make something really unique, like the fantastic two-scarves belt I saw my friend Jan wearing the other day. . . . Stay tuned!

Zoey set herself up at the dining room table with her sewing machine, sketch pad, patterns, and fabric. It was the only place in the house where she could really spread out, and when she had a big project to sew, the dining room became her office. Luckily, her brother and father didn't much care about eating in the dining room and were happy to let Zoey take it over whenever she needed to. With her Etsy store inventory and mailing supplies spread out around the room, it was starting to feel like her very own design studio.

Zoey had made a pretty simple pattern for Kate's dress by combining store-bought shirt and skirt patterns, so she decided to start that dress first. She turned on her sewing machine and began laying out pieces of the pattern over the fabric, so she could start cutting. She always found this part slow and tricky, because pinning the pattern on the fabric properly took a lot of patience, and Jan had told her time and time again to measure twice and cut once. The fabric she'd bought for Kate was expensive, and she hadn't bought enough yards to cover any huge mistakes. Even though she had a larger fabric budget than usual, she didn't want to waste it. So she'd have to go slowly and carefully.

When she finished cutting all the pieces, she pinned them again, so that she'd have guidelines for sewing. When she'd pinned the skirt of the dress, and checked it for any wrinkles or unevenness, she slid what would be the bottom hem of the dress under the feed dog of the machine and placed her foot on the pedal.

Nothing happened. Not a whir, not a buzz, nothing.

That's weird, thought Zoey. She checked over all the settings on the machine and noticed it felt warmer than it usually did. In fact, it felt hot. She turned it off, waited a few minutes to let it cool down, then turned it back on. That trick usually worked with her laptop and her phone. Then she lined up her fabric again, crossed her fingers, and put her foot on the pedal. The sewing machine sprang to life and began stitching.

Zoey heaved a sigh of relief. This was not the time for her mother's old sewing machine to let her down! They had two big jobs to do!

Zoey worked for several minutes, until she noticed that the hem wasn't looking right with the stitches in it. It was pulling as she sewed, and that was distorting the beautiful swirls on the fabric.

She decided to stop and try it a few times on scraps of fabric that were left over from cutting. But no matter how slowly she went, the same thing kept happening.

Zoey was frustrated. She was starting to wonder if it needed to be handled differently. She decided to take a break from Kate's dress for the moment to work on Priti's. After all, she had this other whole project to work on.

She swapped out Kate's pattern and fabric for Priti's, and began laying out and cutting the fabric for Priti's sari. She was thrilled with the sari fabrics she'd chosen to blend together.

Zoey was just starting to make some good progress when Marcus came in and sat down.

"How's it going?" he asked, looking around at Zoey's piles of sewing things covering every surface.

"Fine," said Zoey. "I'm making a sari for Priti. Do you want to see the sketch? It's right here."

"No," he said, shaking his head. "I meant how's it going with the Etsy store."

Zoey looked up, glad she had good news to tell. "Oh, pretty well. I've made a couple of sales! Well, one buyer was Aunt Lulu, but the other buyer is someone I don't know. Actually, I'd better pack that order up tonight. . . . I almost forgot." She bit her lip, realizing she also had forgotten that she still had homework to do. Her dad had seen her sewing earlier and asked if she had finished her homework. Zoey had promised him she would get it done, but her sewing had taken a lot longer than she'd planned.

"That's great, Zo. And how about Allie?" Marcus asked insistently. "I mean, how's she doing? You know, with sales and stuff."

Zoey looked at him oddly. She'd still been thinking about her homework. "Um, she's fine, I guess. I haven't talked to her since the weekend. But she's probably sold some more stuff too."

Marcus nodded. "That's good. I'm glad. You should have her come over again this weekend. You know, to help you with your orders. Or just to hang out, even."

Distracted, Zoey nodded. It was nice Marcus was so interested in her Etsy store, but he clearly didn't understand how much sewing she had to do!

She wouldn't be able to just "hang out" with anyone for another week, at least.

To change the subject, she asked, "Hey, did Dad just go out? I heard him yell something, and then the front door closed, but I was concentrating so hard, I wasn't really paying attention."

"Yeah, he's going out with a woman he met from work. I think he's been out with her before. He yelled that he left us money for pizza."

Zoey's eyes lit up. "Pizza! I'm starving! Will you order it? I really want to get more work done on this before I have to start my math homework." Then she paused. "I'm glad Dad's . . . met someone nice . . . but it still feels weird, doesn't it?"

"Yeah," Marcus replied with a shrug. "But I guess it's a good thing. Any excuse for pizza is a good thing. I'll call in the order."

Marcus got up and left, leaving Zoey to her work. It was really nice having a brother sometimes. Especially one who liked pizza and ice cream as much as she did and didn't mind driving her to fabric stores and having a dining room full of fabric and accessories.

Zoey continued to work on the dresses for the next two days, making only marginal progress. The fabric from Kate's dress was tricky to sew, and it turned out that tulip skirts required a lot of pinning to get right. The sari Zoey designed had so many layers that it was really time-consuming too. She found herself looking longingly at the headbands she'd made for the Etsy site and thinking about how easy they'd been to make. Maybe it wouldn't be bad to be a designer who focused exclusively on accessories. . . .

On Thursday evening, as she was sitting down to sew, her phone rang. Glad for a minute to have something to do besides sew, she answered it.

"It's Libby," said Libby, even though her name appeared on Zoey's phone when she called.

"I know," said Zoey, giggling. "What's up?"

"I just wanted to see how you're doing," Libby answered. "How are the dresses?"

Zoey was relieved Libby asked. She'd been starting to worry she'd never, ever be finished, and she needed someone to talk to about it. "Well, do you think Priti or Kate would mind wearing *half* a dress to their parties? 'Cause that might be all they get!"

"What?" cried Libby. "Why?"

"I'm really worried I'm going to let them down, Libby," Zoey confessed. "Both dresses are turning out to be harder than I thought. Kate might have to wear a tank top with just a skirt! Or maybe a bathing suit as a top."

"She'd probably prefer that!" Libby joked.

Zoey laughed. "You're right! She would." She sighed. "But, seriously, time is ticking, and there aren't many days until Priti leaves for India. And suddenly I've got orders coming in from Etsy to deal with, and not only that, I get tons of e-mails every day with questions from people who *might* want to buy and just want to learn more about each piece. My dad helps, but it takes a while to answer them all too. Some of them want pictures from different angles, all kinds of stuff."

"I could help," Libby offered. "Maybe I could come over this weekend and help you mail things and answer e-mails."

"Oh, would you?" Zoey said. "Thanks, Libby, you're the best!"

"No problem," said Libby.

"I should probably get back to work now," Zoey said. "But thanks for calling. I owe you another dress too. Once I've recovered from these. *If* I recover."

Libby laughed. "You must be okay if you're making jokes. I don't need another dress yet—I still love the Libby dress you made for me. I'd wear it every day if I could!"

"Ha-ha, I dare you. Imagine what Ivy would say if you did!" said Zoey. "Anyway, see you tomorrow."

"See you."

The next day in social studies class, Zoey was trying to listen and take notes while the back of her brain was working on how to get the fabric for Priti's dress to stay over the shoulder just so, while being comfortable *and* easy to take on and off. It was a construction problem, and she didn't have enough sewing experience yet to do it right. Sometimes it seemed like the more she sewed, the more she needed to learn about sewing.

She doodled part of Priti's dress on her notebook, studying it from various perspectives. She still loved the design and didn't want to change it.

Suddenly, she heard someone clear her throat very deliberately. Afraid she'd been caught not listening in class, Zoey looked up guiltily and tried to appear like she'd been listening. But it was just Ivy, who was leaning across the aisle and studying Zoey's little sketch.

"Designing more outfits for customers that pee and poop in the backyard, Zoey?" she asked. "What's next? Outfits for squirrels?"

Before Zoey could even think of a response, her friend Gabe immediately chimed in, "You know, Ivy, most dogs are nicer than *you* are. I know mine is."

Zoey looked at him gratefully as Ivy curled her lip and pulled back to her seat. Gabe was always a good friend to Zoey, helpful and nice. Nicer than a lot of the boys in their grade. And she knew he adored his dog, Mr. Paws, because Gabe kept a picture of him in his locker.

It's a good thing Ivy doesn't know Gabe's dog is

named Mr. Paws, Zoey thought. *Or she'd make fun of that too!*

"And so, class," Mr. Dunn was saying, "if you look at your schedule, you'll see we have our unit test next Friday, which gives you a full week to study. Make sure you go over all the readings from the unit, as well as the exercises we did in class. This will count twenty-five percent toward your grade."

Zoey snapped to attention. *Test? What test?* She looked at her organizer and saw it written there, just after "Priti goes to India!" and right before "Kate's spaghetti dinner!" How on earth would she fit studying into her schedule too?

Zoey was staring gloomily at her day planner when the bell rang and students started to file out of the classroom. Ivy made a soft "woof, woof" sound under her breath as she got up and left, hoping to get a rise out of Zoey, but Zoey didn't have the energy. Who cared what Ivy thought about her Doggie Duds clothes, anyway? *Obviously people liked them,* she thought, *or they wouldn't have contributed to the campaign!*

Gabe gathered his books and paused by Zoey's desk.

"You okay?" he asked. "You don't seem like yourself today."

Zoey shrugged. "I guess so. I just realized I may have overcommitted myself. . . ."

"Oh yeah? How?"

Zoey showed him her calendar and explained about her friends, the dresses, Etsy, and the big test. Just talking about it made her feel a bit jittery.

"Well," said Gabe thoughtfully, "which dress needs to be ready first, and which is the most difficult?"

Zoey hadn't thought about it that way. "Um, Kate's is easier, but Priti's needs to be ready sooner."

Gabe nodded. "I'd finish Kate's dress first, since it's simpler, because you'll feel much better once you get one whole thing out of the way. That's what my mom always says. Then you focus on the next thing."

It was like a lightbulb in Zoey's brain. She'd been trying to do it all at once and make progress on everything every day. Gabe was right—she needed to follow the advice she had given to Priti. *I guess it's not always easy to follow your own advice,* she thought, *but he's right. I think I can do it.* "Thanks, Gabe! You're right. That's a good idea."

Gabe paused for a second, then said, "You know, I could help you study for the social studies test if you want. I mean, since you're going to be so busy."

Gabe really was a nice boy, and Zoey knew it was a good offer.

"Thanks, Gabe," she said. "I'll think about it, okay? But first I'm going to finish Kate's dress!"

Feeling reinvigorated, Zoey went home on Friday, ready to attack Kate's dress. The first thing she did was call Jan at A Stitch in Time to explain the problems she was having with the stretchy knit fabric. Thankfully, Jan knew exactly what to do. She recommended using a zigzag stitch and placing a piece of paper on the top and bottom of the fabric to keep it from stretching while sewing it. She wished Zoey good luck and told her to call her if she had any more questions.

Zoey decided that from then on, when she was

feeling a bit underwater, she needed to tell someone sooner rather than later and to ask for some help!

Why do I waste so much time spinning my wheels? Zoey thought. *I'm surrounded by brilliant people!*

Luckily, Jan's advice worked like a charm. Now that Zoey understood how to work with the fabric, it wasn't so challenging. With no homework due the next day because it was the weekend, she was able to get several hours of sewing in that night and then woke up Saturday morning ready to begin again.

Her father noticed how hard she was working and brought her yummy energy snacks, like celery and peanut butter, to keep her going. Zoey had told him about the big test. When he suggested maybe she was taking on too much sewing and needed to focus on school, Zoey said she felt she could do it, and he said brain food might help.

Still, Zoey couldn't believe that shortly after lunch, she finished making the dress! Hurriedly, she ironed it. She was thrilled with how it had turned out, and she was dying to show Kate. She sent Kate a quick text that she was coming over and then grabbed the dress and ran up the block to Kate's house.

Zoey had been to Kate's home so many times over the years, hundreds probably, that she almost thought of it as her own. That's why she never thought twice about simply shouting hello to Kate's parents when they opened the front door and running up the stairs to Kate's room.

Kate was sitting on her bed, finishing up some homework. When she saw the hanger Zoey was holding, covered with a black garment bag, she jumped up.

"Wow!" said Zoey. "I've never seen you this excited about clothes before! I'm honored."

Kate laughed. "I've never *been* this excited because I've never had a Zoey Webber original dress before! Let me see it—I'm dying!"

Zoey was pleased she'd taken the extra few minutes, even though she was bone-tired, to sew in one of her special Sew Zoey labels. They'd been a gift from her fashion fairy godmother, Fashionsista. Zoey whipped off the bag to reveal the dress, and

Kate's face lit up. "Oh, Zo—it's so *me*! It's perfect!"

She reached out and hugged Zoey hard, and immediately all the hours of work and worry that had gone into making Kate the perfect dress had been worth it. Zoey loved being able to make a friend this happy.

"And now the hard part . . . ," Kate said, shimmying out of her sweatpants. "Trying it on."

"That's not the hard part. The hard part is you've got to *win* your state championships next weekend so that this will be a victory dress," Zoey teased. "Your team will have the best dinner ever!"

Kate pulled the dress over her head and walked to her closet door, where there was a full-length mirror hanging on the other side. She stood quietly for a moment, looking at herself.

Zoey grew anxious. *She* thought the dress looked amazing on Kate. But why was Kate so quiet?

"Don't you . . . don't you like it?" Zoey asked.

Kate turned back toward Zoey and almost looked as if she had tears in her eyes. "I love it," Kate said. "I really, really love it. I've been wearing the same old T-shirts and jeans, and things my mom picked out for so long, and I never really cared about my clothes. I didn't even want anyone to look at me. But I love this dress, and I want everyone to see it!"

The girls hugged again, and there was a quick knock as the door to Kate's bedroom opened. It was Mrs. Mackey, and Zoey got nervous all over again, wondering if Kate's mother would approve the dress.

Kate spun in a circle, showing off the dress for her mother. Then she stood still, with her arms out and her cheeks slightly flushed, and said, "What do you think, Mom?"

Mrs. Mackey's face broke into a huge grin. "Well, my goodness, that's pretty. I think it's a beautiful dress, honey. And I think I have a very, very beautiful daughter."

Then Mrs. Mackey, who had in some ways been like a mother to Zoey, walked over to Zoey and hugged her.

"You're a very talented young lady," Mrs. Mackey said. "I'm so proud of you."

Zoey grinned. She couldn't imagine any feeling better than this. Designing something perfect for one of her best friends in the whole world and having her *and* her mother both love it?

It called for a celebration. Of the ice-cream variety.

"Mrs. Mackey," Zoey began, "do you think maybe Kate and I could go out for ice cream?"

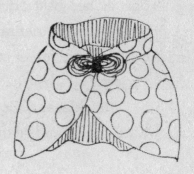

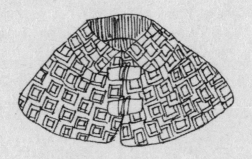

CHAPTER 5

Mistakes, Mistakes, Mistakes . . .

I can hardly believe it, but Kate's dress is done! I had to call some experts for help (thanks, JAN!!!), but I finally finished sewing the spaghetti dress. (I can't help calling it that, even though it's not really spaghetti in the pattern.) I took it over to Kate's this afternoon, and she loved it! I definitely wasted a lot of time this week with sewing errors, and after months of learning to sew, I can't believe I'm still making mistakes like that. But my dad says I need to remember that even for experts, there's always something new to learn. He also asked: How boring would it be if I already knew everything there was to know about sewing at my age? Clearly, that's not a problem for me! (Hee-hee!)

Anyway, here's a sketch of some little capelets I'm thinking of making (someday, if I ever have time). Some what, you ask? Well, the other day I saw a customer of mine (ahem), Buttons the dog, wearing her Doggie Duds outfit, which kind of looks like a cape or swing coat with little sleeves. And she looked soooo cute, I thought I wouldn't mind having a little capelet myself to throw over a shirt or sweater when it starts getting chilly out, but it's not the time of year for a real coat. It could also work as a wrap for a dress!

And speaking of dresses . . . I still need to get cracking on Priti's dress, since she's leaving for India in just a few days, and I have Etsy orders to take care of, AND my huge social studies test on Friday that I need

to study for so, wait, WHY am I still blogging?
    GOOD NIGHT!!!

Sunday morning, Zoey woke up, still feeling somewhat tired but hugely relieved that at least one of her big projects was done. *I really can do it all if I just pace myself,* she thought as she zipped up a hoodie over her pajamas and headed downstairs to her "workroom."

The night before, Zoey had laid out the material for Priti's dress and put everything where it needed to be so she could start sewing quickly without having to set up everything. Her phone buzzed, and she checked it quickly, feeling a mix of happiness and chagrin when she saw that it was another Etsy order. She turned on her sewing machine to let it warm up, and while it did, she quickly fired off answers to two potential Etsy customers. She was nearly sold out on all of her items, which she was beginning to think wasn't such a bad thing. Allie had also sent her an e-mail checking in on how sales were going. It sounded like Allie hadn't sold quite as many things, which made Zoey feel funny, since the pop-up shop had been Allie's idea to begin with.

When the machine was fully warmed up, Zoey mentally went over her new plan for sewing the top half of the dress. Jan had given her advice on how to do it properly, and Zoey followed it to the letter, pinning the fabric carefully. Then she slid the material under the machine's feed dog and hit the pedal. Slowly and carefully, she sewed, stopping frequently to make sure she was following Jan's advice, so the fabric wouldn't pinch or pleat anywhere.

She'd been working about a half an hour when the sewing machine made a loud noise, like a *whirr-whirr-THUNK*, jammed up with a nest of tangled thread, and stopped cold. Zoey put her hand on the machine and it felt red hot.

No, no, NO! Not again! Zoey thought.

Quickly, she turned the machine off and let it cool down, then hit the button to turn it back on, as she'd done before when it had given her problems. But this time it wouldn't even turn back on.

"Mom's machine!" Zoey moaned. "How can

this be happening?" Zoey resisted giving the old machine a whack with her hand, which is what her dad did when the laundry machine acted up. The sewing machine was more than twenty years old, she knew, maybe even twenty-five, and it had been working very hard lately.

Zoey was looking over Priti's half-sewn dress and sighing when her brother and father came downstairs. Marcus was yawning, his eyes still half-closed, and didn't see her, but Zoey's father noticed right away that something was wrong.

"Zoey, what is it?" her father asked. "And why are you up so early?"

Zoey buried her head in her hands. She didn't want to tell her father that the machine that had been so special to her mother was broken. But she had to.

"Dad, Mom's machine broke!" she admitted mournfully. "It was acting up every once in a while, but now it *really* broke. I don't know what to do!"

She hoped he wouldn't be mad at her. She didn't think she could take it.

Mr. Webber came over to the dining room table

immediately and stood for a second, rubbing Zoey's shoulders. Then he said, "There, there, Zo. It's just a machine. We can get it fixed."

Marcus looked fully awake now, and appeared upset about his mom's old machine. "But it's so old, Dad. They might not even make parts for it anymore."

Zoey covered her face with both hands.

"That's not very helpful, Marcus," Mr. Webber said calmly. "Why don't you go start the pancakes, and I'll take a look at the machine."

"Okay," Marcus agreed, heading into the kitchen. "Sorry, Zoey."

"It's okay," she muttered, because she knew Marcus hadn't meant to be harsh. He was just telling the truth.

"It couldn't have happened at a worse time, either, Dad," Zoey said as her father opened a panel on the machine to look at its insides.

He tinkered with it a moment, then closed it back up. "I'll find a repair place this week, Zoey. Don't worry—they might be able to do something with it. Plus, school comes first, and even though

I'm sure you're brilliant, you still need to study for that test. But come in the kitchen now and have some pancakes. Things always look brighter after a good breakfast."

Zoey got up and followed her dad into the kitchen, where Marcus already had made the batter. He began pouring heaping spoonfuls onto the skillet. The Webbers had a family tradition of making pancakes every weekend with different secret ingredients each time they cooked. Whoever wasn't cooking had to guess what was inside.

But Zoey didn't have the heart to care about this week's secret ingredient. She plopped down at the kitchen table and couldn't help moaning again. Her dad started setting out napkins and silverware.

"What now, Zo?" Marcus asked.

"Well," she said, "I promised Priti I'd make her a sari for her cousin's wedding in India, but she leaves *Wednesday*, and now the machine is broken. *And*, I have a bunch of Etsy orders I need to get packed and shipped, and I have to update the site and answer questions. Libby was going to come over and help me today, but she forgot she has to study for the ginormous social studies test we have on Friday, which, by the way, I also have to study for."

"Yikes," said Marcus. "That's a crummy week."

"Thanks," sad Zoey drily. "Thanks a lot."

Marcus shrugged, a big-brotherly smirk on his face. "C'mon, I didn't mean it like that. I could help with the Etsy orders if you want. Invite Allie over. We could all do it together."

"That would be fun," Zoey replied, "but I don't know. I'd feel weird asking her to help me pack up things I've sold."

"Well, I'll help, Zoey," her dad offered, "so it will be done and you can focus on schoolwork. But first let's eat these pancakes, which are a strange, brownish color today, Marcus. What did you do to them?"

Marcus smiled mysteriously.

Zoey picked up one of the hot, steaming pancakes and sniffed it. "Hershey's chocolate syrup?" she guessed, taking a big bite. "Yep. And some dried strawberries, I think. Deeeeeelicious."

"You really have a knack for this, Zo," Marcus

said. "You should add pro pancake taster to your list of talents. You got it!"

It turned out Mr. Webber was right. Everything looked brighter after a breakfast of chocolatey pancakes.

With her sewing materials, also known as Priti's sari, all over the dining room, Mr. Webber, Marcus, and Zoey moved all the Etsy stuff to the living room and created an assembly line to get the products packed, checked, labeled, and ready for the post office. Zoey answered Etsy e-mails while her father and brother managed the orders, and after just a short while, Zoey felt like they'd made huge progress.

"Thanks, you guys," Zoey said gratefully. "You might just be the best family in the entire world."

"I'm definitely the best *brother* in the entire world," Marcus said confidently as he carefully wrapped a headband in tissue paper. "Just don't tell anyone I spent the morning playing with hair doodads and purses."

"I won't," Zoey said, laughing. "I promise."

"So do you feel better, then, Zo?" her father asked.

Zoey let out a huge sigh. "Well, sort of. The problem is, I still want to make this sari for Priti. I know she'd love it! And *I* would love to know that one of my dresses is being worn at a wedding in India! But I just don't know how I can get it done in such a short time . . . without my machine. I'll try sewing it by hand, but I don't know if I can."

"So talk to Priti," her dad suggested. "Tell her your machine broke. She's your friend, honey—she'll understand."

Zoey nodded. "You're right. I will. I'll call her later and tell her the whole story."

The three of them continued working for a few minutes until Mr. Webber said, "Zoey, you *still* have a frown on your face. Is something *else* bothering you, too?"

Zoey felt guilty. Her whole family was helping her, and using their Sunday to do it, and she was still worrying about finishing Priti's dress. But the thing that was worrying her most at that moment wasn't even about her to-do list.

"Dad," Zoey began, "I think I've sold more stuff than Allie has in our pop-up shop. And I feel really bad about it, because it was *her* idea, and she's been doing this longer, and *she's* the one that e-mailed TresChic.com about us and stuff. If it weren't for her, I wouldn't even be *doing* this!"

Marcus looked concerned, and her dad came and sat beside her. "Don't worry about things you can't control, Zoey. Maybe you sold more this week, but she might sell a lot more next week. It'll all even out, I'm sure. In the meantime, just be a good business partner. Promote your joint site. Be supportive. Okay?"

Zoey nodded. Her dad made a lot of sense.

"Allie seems like a pretty cool girl," Marcus added. "I wouldn't worry too much. Also, she's in high school. She's busy. I doubt she's obsessing about who sold more of what."

For the first time that morning, Zoey's face broke into a huge smile. Yes, things were hectic at the moment, but it would all work out. Suddenly, she remembered an interview she'd read recently on TresChic.com with her favorite designer,

Daphne Shaw. Daphne had said, "Sometimes I get overwhelmed thinking about how much I have to do before a show. But instead of panicking, I just put my head down and sew. And I try to remember that when I'm really, really busy. Just to put my head down and sew, sew, sew."

It was good advice, and Zoey would take it. Just as soon as her sewing machine was fixed. Later that day, she cracked open her social studies textbook and tried to study, but mostly she stared at the pages blankly. Then she *did* put her head down—on the book—and slept, slept, slept.

CHAPTER 6

Broken Machine, Broken Heart

Something so awful has happened, I almost can't even blog about it! But I have to, because it's huge and it's messing up everything. My mother's old sewing machine is broken! ☹ I mean completely broken. I can't even get it to turn on. I feel like I'm stranded in the jungle without it. My dad says I have to "stay calm and sew on," and he's promised to find a local repair shop that specializes in old machines like mine to fix it, but deep down I'm worried that maybe it can't be fixed. And without it I'm not sure how I will be able to sew my friend Priti's sari in time for her trip!

In the meantime, I did manage to send off all my Etsy orders, which is a huge relief. (Thanks, Dad and Marcus, for your help!) Not to mention, as you can see from this sketch, when I was thinking about jungles, I came up with a pretty cool idea for a—drumroll, please—CARGO DRESS! Cargo pants and cargo shorts are so practical for being able to stow things in your pockets, right? But what if you want something a little more fashion forward that still gives you options? That's right—you want a cargo dress! This would be perfect for me on weekends, when I'm not carrying my backpack but want to bring my sketchbook, pen, and wallet with me when I go somewhere. In particular, when I go to some of Dad's teams' games at the university and don't want to carry a bag I might lose in the stands. I would love to make this in time for the next game, but it'll have to wait until I have more time, and a working sewing machine . . . SEW frustrating. But thanks for listening, folks!

Please send your positive, healing thoughts to my sewing machine!

Zoey hit the button to publish her blog post. With that done, she decided it was time to call Priti and tell her the news about the machine. Priti would find out when she read the blog, anyway. Zoey knew Priti would be understanding—she always was. Zoey just hated the idea of letting down one of her best friends. And she was afraid she would be.

Zoey picked up her phone and dialed Priti's number. Priti answered on the first ring.

"Hi, Zoey! Long time no talk. What have you been up to this weekend, like I can't guess?" Priti sounded as upbeat and perky as ever. She apparently hadn't checked Zoey's blog in the last five minutes.

"Um, just sewing, obviously, and you know, doing the Etsy stuff. I finished Kate's dress."

"I know!" Priti exclaimed. "I read your blog yesterday, and then Kate called me last night and told me how much she loved it. Yay! I can't wait to see it in person. It's made me even more excited for my sari!"

Inwardly, Zoey groaned. Why, oh why, did her machine have to break?

"Priti, I have to tell you something," she began. "My sewing machine broke this morning, and it isn't working at all. It won't even turn *on*."

"Oh no, really?" Priti paused. "Your mom's machine . . . Oh, Zo, I'm so sorry! You must be so upset!"

Zoey nodded, even though Priti couldn't see her. "I am, *very*. My dad is going to try and find a place that fixes old machines, but it will probably take some time, and time is something we don't have much of before you leave for India. . . . And I just don't know if I can . . . well, I'm not sure if . . ."

Zoey let her voice trail off, still unable to tell her friend she might not be able to finish making the dress that she'd promised her.

But Priti, ever the good friend, knew exactly what Zoey wasn't saying. "It's okay, Zoey. I totally understand. Don't worry about it, okay?"

Zoey let out a huge sigh of relief. Priti could always be counted on to be sunny and optimistic, even when she was probably really, really disappointed.

"Let me just tell my mom, okay?" Priti said. "Hang on . . ."

Zoey heard Priti shout to her mother that the sari Zoey was supposed to be making her might not be ready in time for the wedding.

Then she heard Mrs. Holbrooke yell back, "What sari that Zoey's making? Your grandmother is bringing a sari for you. The one she wore when she was your age. Didn't I tell you? She would be so touched if you wear it."

Zoey heard Priti gasp. "Mom, what *are* you talking about? I told you all about Zoey's design, remember? And you said she could make it! She's been working soooooo hard on it!"

Zoey felt embarrassed, and she wished she weren't overhearing the conversation.

Then Zoey heard Mrs. Holbrooke yell back, "Oh my goodness. I'm so sorry, Priti. I do remember something about that. I've just been a little preoccupied lately and completely forgot, and when your grandmother mentioned her old sari, I thought it would be perfect for you. I thought I'd told you about it last week . . . but maybe I didn't. Poor Zoey."

There was a long pause, and Zoey realized maybe this wasn't such a bad thing after all. Priti would have a dress to wear, and Zoey wouldn't have to kill herself trying to handsew a sari by Wednesday.

"PRITI!" Zoey yelled into her phone.

She heard some scrabbling noises, and Priti picked up her cell again. "Yeah? I guess you heard that, right?" she asked glumly.

"I did," admitted Zoey, "but it's okay. It's totally fine if you wear your grandmother's dress, because I don't know how I'd finish . . ."

Priti cut her off. "Hold on. Let me go to my room so we can talk." Zoey heard Priti's footsteps and a door closing. "Okay, thanks. I just don't know what's going on with my mother lately," she whispered into the phone. "I mean, she and my dad were seeing a counselor for a while, and things had started to get better, at least that's what my sisters and I thought, but the past few weeks my mom has been all distant and distracted. Like, a total space cadet. Do you think they're having trouble again?"

Zoey's heart ached for her friend. She could hear in Priti's voice how upset she was. She knew how much Priti had worried about her parents recently, and that she had hoped the upcoming family trip abroad would be a fun way for them all to enjoy being together, like they used to.

"I don't know, Priti," Zoey said. "But I hope not."

"They've been fighting a lot," Priti said, her voice still low. *"Loudly."*

"I'm so sorry," Zoey said. She knew she couldn't relate to living with parents arguing, since she'd only had one parent for most of her life, and her father was always so easygoing, anyway. Even she and Marcus hardly fought the way brothers and sisters sometimes did. There just wasn't much fighting in the Webber house. But she knew Priti needed support, and Zoey would try to help in whatever way she could.

"I'm always here if you want to talk," Zoey offered. "Or come over. Or spend the night. Or make chocolate *chocolate*-chip cookies," she joked.

Priti half laughed. "Thanks, Zoey."

"They were really good cookies."

Priti laughed again, then, sounding falsely cheerful, added, "It'll all be okay. I just loved the design for the sari you did, Zoey. It's so beautiful. I hate for it to go to waste."

Zoey felt terrible for her friend, who seemed to be dealing with so much and doing it so bravely. It made it easy to say, "You know, Priti, I'm going to try really hard to have it ready by the time you leave. But if I can't finish it in time for this wedding, I'll finish it soon, just so you'll have it. Maybe you can wear it to another wedding."

"What?" exclaimed Priti. "But you don't have to, Zoey . . . and you don't even have a *machine*!"

"It's okay," Zoey said. "I'll handsew it. You deserve it, Priti."

"Thanks, Zo."

Priti sighed deeply, but it was a sigh of delight and relief. Zoey felt a warm spot in her chest, knowing she was at least doing *something* to make her friend a tiny bit happier.

CHAPTER 7

Tick-Tock, Tick-Tock!

It's funny how normally the only reason I even know what day it is is because of my class schedule at school. But for the past week or so, I've known exactly what MINUTE of the hour it is, all day long! That's what happens when you're trying to get a lot done—fast!

So, no good news on my sewing machine yet. I've decided that even if it can't be fixed ☹, I'm going to keep it in my room forever, because it was my mother's and I learned how to sew on it. It'll be like a vintage fashion sculpture. ☺ In the meantime, I'm going to have to figure out how to make some money (selling more accessories, maybe?) to buy myself a new machine! I'm guessing it'll take a while. . . .

Until then, I'm working hard to finish Priti's sari (by hand!) before she leaves for India on Wednesday, and I have to say, it is really turning out beautifully. I'm not posting a picture, because I don't want to ruin the surprise for Priti. (HA! I know you're reading this, P!)

In other design-y news, I've become such a sewing EXPERT on stretchy fabrics recently that I got an idea for a bathing suit for myself for summer! This sketch is still not finished, but I'm posting it, anyway. And I also attached a sketch for a little stretchy sundress. Hoping for sunnier days ahead!

In the hallway at school Tuesday morning, Priti pulled Zoey aside by the lockers. She looked nervous, which wasn't how Zoey was used to seeing Priti look. It made Zoey wonder if something had happened with her parents.

"Priti, what it is?" Zoey asked. "Are you okay?"

Priti sensed the panic in Zoey's voice. "Yeah, yeah—I'm okay. It's just that, well, the more I think about it, the more I want to wear my grandmother's special dress." She paused, eyeing Zoey guiltily. "I know it'll mean a lot to my mom, and she's having a hard time right now with . . . you know . . . everything."

Zoey nodded. She knew what Priti meant.

Priti looked down at the floor. "Do you hate me? I know you've gone to so much trouble to handsew the sari, and you're probably almost done, and here I am telling you I might not want to wear it. . . ."

Much to Zoey's surprise, she felt relieved. She *wasn't* finished sewing the sari, not even close, and she was still really overwhelmed with schoolwork and the new Etsy orders trickling in. She could always finish the sari for Priti to wear to something else in the future.

"It's *fine*, Priti," Zoey said, putting her hand on Priti's shoulder. "Honestly. It's no big deal, okay? I'm actually relieved. I don't know if I could have gotten it done in time."

Priti sighed with relief. "Thanks, Zo. I can always count on you to understand."

Zoey shrugged modestly, and then laughed. "Well, I *am* very understanding."

Priti laughed too, and Zoey delighted for a moment in the relief of having one less thing to do. It reminded her there was something she'd been meaning to ask Priti about.

"Hey, Priti," she said in a low voice. "You know what's weird? My brother has been superunderstanding lately too, and, like, really involved with all my sewing stuff. He keeps telling me to invite Allie over and asking me about her and our site. It's like he's interested in fashion all of a sudden!"

Priti's eyes went wide, and she clapped a hand over her mouth to keep from laughing. "Zoey!" she said, her eyes twinkling. "He's not interested in *fashion*, he's interested in Allie! Didn't you say she's in high school too, and very pretty?"

"Yeah, but . . ." Zoey paused, turning the idea over in her mind. Marcus *had* been unusually shy around Allie. And offered to take them both out for ice cream. And asked when she was coming over again. . . .

"Holy cow, you're right!" Zoey exclaimed. "How'd I miss that? I just never thought Marcus would have a crush on one of *my* friends, you know? Ewwww. I mean, I know he liked this girl Grace for a while, but I wasn't *friends* with her. Again, *ewww*!"

Priti shook her head. "It's not *ewww*. It's perfectly normal. People meet, they like each other, they fall in loooooove, they get married and have a big wedding."

At the thought of weddings, Priti's face suddenly tensed up again, and she started to bite her lip nervously.

"What's wrong?" Zoey asked, wondering if Priti was thinking of her own parents' marriage. "I've never seen you frown this much, ever."

Priti sighed and ran one finger down the locker beside her. "Well, the truth is, I'd really like to wear *both* saris to my cousin's wedding, but I don't see how that's possible. Right? That doesn't make sense, even. My mom wants me to wear my grandmother's sari, and I kind of do too. But do you think . . . do you think maybe you could keep working on getting the other sari made in time for the wedding? Just in case I find a time to wear it?"

Zoey felt her stomach flop over. She had been so close to having one less HUGE thing on her plate! But she couldn't say no to Priti, not when she was so obviously upset about her parents. Even with the social studies test coming up faster and faster. And, despite how much work it was to sew, Zoey loved the sari. It was one of her all-time favorite designs! She *wanted* to finish it.

Then, just as Zoey was about to tell Priti yes, she felt her phone buzz in her backpack.

Probably more Etsy orders, Zoey thought. *Greeeeeat.*

Sweating slightly, Zoey assured Priti she would do her best to finish the dress by the next afternoon, just in time for Priti to head to the airport for the flight to India. Priti gave her the world's biggest hug and thanked her a zillion times. Zoey kept a smile on her face, even though inside she was feeling more than a little frantic.

Zoey rushed to her next class, worrying yet again about how she'd be able to finish the sari that night and completely forgetting about the message on her phone. When she finally had a chance to check her phone on the way to lunch, she saw that, in fact, she *had* gotten another order from Etsy, and it was from Libby's aunt! Score!

Even better, it came with a message.

Zoey hurriedly clicked through the e-mail alert and read:

Dear Zoey,

I'm so impressed with the pop-up store you and Allie have created! You truly have some one-of-a-kind accessories here. If you're interested, I'd love to take you both to the crafts and accessories trade show the weekend after next. You can help me "scope out" the aisles for new things to feature at H. Cashin's! Get permission from your parents and let me know if you can make it!

Best,
Alexandra Van Langen
(Libby's aunt)

Zoey read through the message twice and could hardly keep from jumping up and down and shouting. Libby's aunt liked her designs! *And* she wanted to take her and Allie to a real trade show! It was more good news than Zoey could even wish for.

Zoey began to race toward the lunchroom, anxious to tell her friends. On the way, she found Libby and couldn't help shrieking and hugging her.

"What's this for?" Libby asked, laughing. "Did you find out the social studies test is canceled or something?"

"I wish," said Zoey. "No, better. I just got an e-mail from your aunt about the trade show! Did you know?"

Libby nodded. "She just e-mailed me and invited me too. We're all going to go together!"

"Really? Wow!" Zoey's face broke into a smile that was a mile wide. It would be an unforgettable day, and she'd get to share it with Allie *and* Libby.

All she had to do was get through the next few days.

Zoey was still beaming in social studies class that afternoon. She hadn't been so excited for something in a long time. Just thinking about how much she'd learn, walking around a huge trade show like that with Libby's aunt, a *real* buyer from one of the biggest department stores in the country, made her heart leap. It would be like a master class in fashion buying!

"Hey, why are you looking so happy?" Gabe asked. He'd gone up to hand in some homework and caught sight of Zoey's face on his way back to his seat.

Zoey told him briefly about the trade show. Then she added, "Of course, my dad probably won't let me go if I flunk this test on Friday, which I *still* haven't really studied for, because I'm *still* sewing that sari for Priti."

Zoey shook her head woefully. Normally, she didn't mind Mr. Dunn's class, but right now it was giving her a great, big headache!

Gabe toed the floor with one of his sneakers. "You know, Zoey, I could still come over to help you study on Thursday, if you want. I've already been studying some."

Zoey looked at Gabe gratefully. "Oh, Gabe, that's *so* nice of you! I really appreciate it. But I just can't add one more thing to my schedule right now! Even if it's a *really* smart study partner. I'm going to have to figure this out on my own."

Looking down at the ground, Gabe shrugged and said, "Sure, yeah, of course. It was just a thought. Good luck studying, okay?"

"Thanks." Zoey smiled at him again, and Gabe returned to his seat.

Ivy had been listening to the whole conversation and leaned toward Zoey.

"Hey, Zoey. You might want to make *him* one of your little Doggie Duds outfits too," she whispered loudly, "because he follows you around like a puppy!"

Ivy burst into laughter at her own joke, and Zoey felt her cheeks go scarlet. She wished she could think of something terrific and biting to say to Ivy in return, but she couldn't. She was never good at snappy comebacks. And she was mortified that Gabe might have heard. He was being so nice to her, and she really did like him as a friend, at least.

To Zoey's relief, Mr. Dunn cleared his throat to begin class, and Zoey tried to block out Ivy and her mean comment and listen to his lecture. But Ivy's words kept playing in her ears, over and over. Was she treating Gabe badly? Was she not being as good a friend to him as he'd always been to her? She wasn't sure. And the truth was, at the moment, she really didn't have time to think about it. She resolved to do something nice for him as soon as the test was over. What that would be, exactly, she'd worry about later. One thing at a time.

That night, as Zoey was sewing away on the sari, Priti called.

Zoey answered. "Hello, hello, famous sari maker here!"

Priti giggled. "Guess what, Zo?!"

Zoey's heart stuck in her throat. She wasn't sure

she could take another change of plans! "What?" she asked.

"My mom and I came up with an idea! I'm going to wear my grandmother's vintage sari to the traditional wedding ceremony, and then I'm going to wear the sari you're making to the big reception afterward! So your beautiful sari will get to go to India and party, party, party!"

Zoey, whose hands were already cramping from the sewing, sighed with relief for her friend, whom she knew had been stressed about not getting to wear the new sari. If it were anyone but Priti, Zoey might lose it, but for her wonderful, devoted friend, she would sew all night long, finish the sari, and deliver it on time.

"That's awesome news, Priti," Zoey said, and meant it. "I'll finish it tonight, press it, and bring it to you first thing tomorrow at school!"

"YAY!" yelled Priti. "I can't wait! We're leaving straight for the airport after school, so that'll be perfect. I'm sure it'll be amazing!!"

"It better be," joked Zoey, who looked at the clock, trying to figure out how she'd get it finished *and* do her homework. "Now I've gotta go so I can get it done. And you need to pack! Make sure you send me a postcard."

"I will!" promised Priti. "Happy sewing!"

Priti hung up, and Zoey looked at the pile of the mostly finished dress around her. She could do it; she knew she could. It would just be a very, very, *very* long night.

CHAPTER 8

I Survived!

I haven't posted in a few days, which I think is a record for me! But as my loyal readers know, I had a pretty good reason! I finished Priti's sari in the wee, wee hours of Wednesday morning, and she and her family left for India later that day. I haven't heard from her yet, but she tried it on in the bathroom at school, and she looked amaaaazing! Way too pretty to be hanging out in the math hall bathroom, that's for sure. Then my wonderful, thoughtful friend Libby surprised me last night by coming over to help me study for today's social studies test! She even made me some flashcards. I think you know you have a good friend when they go to all the trouble of making you special flashcards. . . . (xo, Libby!) The big test is over, thank goodness, which is a huge relief no matter what grade I get on it.

Really, I could never manage my "double life" (as Dad calls it) of school and being a kid and designing and sewing and all that goes with it, without the help of my awesome family and friends. And that's never been more true than in the past two weeks! I am SEW lucky! One friend in particular, who shall remain nameless, was especially nice and offered to help me several times recently. I need to find a way to thank him (yep, him), and soon!

During my study period today at school, I started thinking about this weekend and how, for once, I have NO SEWING to do. So I was thinking about what I would do with all my free time, and I made a sketch of what

I'd like to spend the weekend wearing—as you can see, it's a ROBE! I've never made one before, and I don't even think I've owned one since I was about seven. But doesn't this one look chic? I bought a splashy, silky print fabric a few weeks ago with my Duds money, and it made me think of a kimono. As soon as I have a new machine—um? Someday?—I'm going to whip this up!

On Saturday morning, Zoey woke up nervous. For once, though, it *wasn't* about sewing or school! It was the day of the soccer state championships. Even though Zoey didn't have to do anything that day other than watch the game, Kate would be playing, and she and her team had been training extra hard for weeks and weeks and weeks. And Zoey knew a little something about working extra hard for a few weeks! Not only that, she and Kate had been such good friends for so long that if one of them was having a big day, they both were. Zoey knew she'd be watching every pass and kick with her heart in her throat, hoping Kate's team would win.

Zoey ate a late breakfast with her brother and

father, and was relieved when Libby came over to go with them to the game. Libby's calm, sweet disposition made her the perfect companion.

"I wish Priti could be here too," Libby said wistfully as they arrived at the stadium.

Zoey nodded. "I know. But her family is probably having a great time traveling around India right now. They have a whole week just to go sightseeing before the wedding! I wish my dad would take Marcus and me on a cool trip like that."

Libby smiled. "Me too. But we *do* have the trade show next weekend to look forward to . . ."

Zoey clapped. "Yes! It'll be the best day ever!"

Mr. Webber, who was scouting the stands for good seats, motioned to Zoey and Libby to join him on a bench. They did quickly as the game was about to start. Zoey saw Kate on the field, and was, as always, struck by how different Kate seemed when she was on the field rather than off it.

When the girls were alone, or at school, Kate was kind of quiet. She didn't make loud jokes or call attention to herself. But when swimming or playing soccer or doing anything on a team, she seemed to come alive. She stood taller, appeared more confident, and seemed so sure of herself. It made Zoey happy to watch. She couldn't wait to see Kate in the spaghetti dress, heading off to her dinner tomorrow night!

"Woo-hooo! Go, Kate!" Zoey yelled.

Kate looked up and waved, then quickly focused her eyes back on the field.

Two girls faced off for the kickoff, and the game began. The two teams were well-matched, and it was a nail-biting game. Kate's team did a great job getting the ball down the field, and Kate, who played left forward, had several opportunities to score. But the opposing team's goalie was really amazing and managed to block nearly every shot.

Zoey and Libby yelled themselves hoarse. Even Mr. Webber, who spent most of his time attending university-level games, was impressed with the level of playing and kept yelling for Kate and her team. Zoey knew that Mr. Webber thought of Kate as an almost-member of the family. She was sure he felt as nervous and excited for Kate's team as she did.

Finally, both teams managed to get on the board, and the score was 2–2, with only a minute left to play. Zoey and Libby were standing up, with the rest of the crowd in the stadium, chanting and yelling for their team. With only seconds left, someone passed the ball to Kate, who deftly dribbled the ball past opponents and raced to the goal. A girl from the other team stole the ball, and Kate charged her, sliding to regain control of the ball and kicking it, nearly upside down, to shoot right into the goal.

The goalie lunged for it but missed. Kate scored the winning goal!

The crowd went wild, and Libby, Zoey, and Mr. Webber jumped up and down and hugged one another. Then they rushed to the field to congratulate Kate on her amazing performance.

But Kate, glowing from the rush of scoring the winning goal, was still lying on the field. As her friends and teammates approached her, Kate started to get up slowly. Mr. Webber was the first to get to Kate, and he held out his hand to give her a high five. But as soon as Kate raised her right arm to high-five him back, she cried out. Her cheeks went from pink to white, and Zoey knew immediately that Kate was in a lot of pain.

"Uh-oh," said Mr. Webber. "Easy, Kate, let's get a look at that arm. If it's injured, it's going to start hurting more as your adrenalin wears off."

Mr. Webber flagged down the medical team, and they raced over to Kate. Mr. Webber made her lie back down, and the team checked her over carefully while Zoey, and Kate's parents, who had just run onto the field as well, stood back and looked on anxiously.

Zoey and Libby held hands and waited for the verdict.

The medical team spoke quietly with Zoey's dad; while beneath them, Kate sat, looking small and pale. Her arm had been wrapped and placed in a sling.

The medical team went to Kate's parents and began talking to them, and Mr. Webber came over to Libby and Zoey.

"She's okay," he said quickly when he saw how worried the girls were. "It's just a sprained elbow. It hurts a lot, but it's going to heal up fine in a few weeks. She needs a lot of rest and can't play any sports for the time being, but she's okay."

Zoey breathed a huge sigh of relief. A sprain. That didn't sound too terrible. She ducked low, so she could catch Kate's eye as the medical team prepared to help her off the field and get her to the locker room for ice and elevation. Kate saw her and gave Zoey a brave smile and a wave with her good arm.

Are you okay? Zoey mouthed.

Kate nodded. *We won!* she mouthed back, managing a wide smile, despite the pain.

Zoey knew then that Kate would be just fine. The Mackeys followed Kate and the medical team back to the locker room, and Mr. Webber suggested he take Zoey and Libby home. They could call Kate later that afternoon, after she'd had some rest and was feeling better.

Zoey took a quick picture of the final scoreboard score with her phone, so she could send it to Kate later. She knew Kate liked to keep mementos from her games in an album, the way Zoey liked to take pictures of some of the outfits she came up with, so she wouldn't forget them.

"That was quite a game," Zoey said to Libby as they left the stadium.

"I'll say. I didn't know soccer was so . . . dangerous!" Libby replied.

Zoey texted back and forth with Kate a few times later that day, until Mrs. Mackey took Kate's phone away to force her to get some rest. Zoey ate dinner with her brother and father and tried not to worry about her friend. She almost wished she had some sewing to do to distract herself! She answered Etsy e-mails and checked in with Allie, who had sold several things during the week and was feeling really good about their pop-up store.

Sunday morning, after Zoey was cleaning up her family's regular pancake breakfast (secret ingredients: blueberries, and buttermilk steeped with rosemary!), the family's home phone rang. Zoey ran to grab it, wondering who it could be.

"Hello?" she said.

"Hi, Zoey. It's Kate's mom," said Mrs. Mackey. "How are you?"

"Fine," Zoey answered, somewhat anxiously. Why was Mrs. Mackey, instead of Kate, calling her? Had something happened? "Is Kate all right?"

"Yes, yes," said Mrs. Mackey. "Well, she's upset about not being able to do anything athletic for a few weeks, but she is feeling better today and slept pretty well last night. That's why I'm calling."

She paused, and Zoey waited, still not quite understanding why Mrs. Mackey had called her.

"You see, I really want Kate to be able to attend the big dinner tonight, and she's *dying* to wear the dress you made for her. But because it's a T-shirt top, it needs to be pulled on over her head, and Kate can't raise her arm at all right now! I checked her closet for something sleeveless to wear, but Kate refuses to wear anything but the beautiful dress you made for her."

Zoey felt flattered once again that Kate cared so much about the spaghetti dress. And she totally understood that after getting so excited to wear one particular outfit, Kate wouldn't want to wear one of the dresses she had already worn—and that her mother had picked out—instead.

"Don't worry, Mrs. Mackey," Zoey said. "I can fix the dress so Kate can put it on without hurting her arm."

"You can?" asked Mrs. Mackey. "But how?"

Zoey didn't know that herself yet. But she knew her friend had scored the winning goal for her team's state championship, and she deserved to wear the dress of her dreams to their team dinner!

"I don't know yet, but I'll find a way," she assured Kate's mom. "I'll come over now and say hi to Kate and pick up the dress. Okay?"

Mrs. Mackey exhaled with relief. "Thank you, Zoey. You have always been so good to my Kate! Come on over, but she's asleep right now so you might have to wait until later to talk to her. I won't tell her yet that you're going to try to fix the dress, just in case it doesn't work out. And if it does, it'll be a wonderful surprise!"

Zoey agreed, and they hung up. As she ran upstairs to change out of her pajamas and race over to Kate's, she thought how funny it was that on her self-proclaimed weekend of "no sewing," here she was, planning a total redesign of a dress, and still without a working sewing machine!

As she started up the street toward Kate's house, her mind was buzzing with ideas on how to make the dress work.

Kate was sleeping when Zoey arrived at the Mackey house, so Zoey returned home soon after she left, with Kate's dress in tow. Zoey set herself up in the dining room, even though she'd be handsewing whatever changes she needed to make to the top of the dress. She liked having the space to spread out that the dining room table gave her, and she liked having her brother and father occasionally walk by to check in on her. One day, when she had her own fashion design office, she'd make sure it was either a shared space with other designers, or right next to some other offices, because seeing and talking to people while she worked gave her energy.

Zoey studied the T-shirt top of the dress and thought hard. She could put in zipper up the back of the dress, but this style of dress really wouldn't look right with a zipper. Not only that, it was awfully hard to do without a sewing machine. She debated taking off the sleeves and making the armholes bigger, more like a crew-neck tank top. She knew she had to make the armholes as large as possible, so Kate could get her swollen arm through. But a tank top with large armholes didn't sound very fancy! And it didn't really look that different from the tank tops Kate usually wore with shorts. She wanted this dress to feel special.

She stared at the beautiful, spaghetti-like print on the skirt. And suddenly it hit her. Spaghetti straps! That would work perfectly! She could make them so that they buttoned on in the back, beneath the shirt fabric, where no one would see them. Kate could easily wiggle the dress on up from the floor, without moving her arm, and then have the straps button over her shoulders. Not only that, the amount of handsewing this change called for wouldn't be that difficult at all!

Zoey immediately set to work, thrilled she'd come up with something that worked with both the short amount of time she had and with the spirit of the dress Kate loved. She finished fairly quickly, and, feeling inspired, went to her room to retrieve some of the extra spaghetti fabric. After some strategizing, and turning the fabric leftovers this way and that, she figured out a way to turn it into a matching sling for Kate to wear, so that she wouldn't have to clutter up her beautiful dress with that wretched hospital-blue sling she'd been given. The matching sling would be the icing on the cake! Or the meatball on the spaghetti!

When both items were finished, Zoey hung the dress on a hanger and, feeling elated with what she'd been able to do in only an afternoon, left for Kate's house.

All of my speed-sewing lately has really paid off! she thought. *I'm almost ready to be on my favorite design show,* Fashion Showdown, *as a contestant.*

Kate was surprised when Zoey arrived and handed her the remade dress. Kate's eyes lit up, and despite looking slightly tired from her injury, Zoey could see she was really feeling much better.

Mrs. Mackey came up to admire the design as well, and Kate tried it on. Mrs. Mackey helped button the new straps in the back and turned Kate around toward the mirror.

"What do you think?" Zoey asked anxiously.

Kate smiled so wide, Zoey could see her molars. "I actually like it even better than the original! And the matching sling cover is perfect. How'd you think of that?"

Zoey shrugged, pleased she'd been able to come through for her friend. It had been a hectic and busy day of sewing, but, as usual, it was worth it when she saw the results.

"Have a great time at the dinner tonight," Zoey said. "Send me lots of pictures! I wish I could be there to clap for the team's star player."

Kate blushed and kept admiring her dress in the mirror. "It's going to be a great night!" she said.

Mrs. Mackey patted her on the shoulder. "Spaghetti straps and a spaghetti pattern for a spaghetti dinner!" she said. "I really can't imagine anything better."

CHAPTER 9

On Top of Spaghetti

Even the best designs don't work out sometimes . .
. like when your best friend sprains her ELBOW scoring
the winning goal at the state championships (!) and
she can't lift her arm over her head to put on her new
made-for-the-occasion Zoey Webber dress! As you can

imagine, this created some problems! Kate was dying to wear the spaghetti dress I'd made, but its T-shirt top with no zipper meant she couldn't put it on with her arm in a sling.

Enter Plan B . . . I picked up the dress this morning and had to come up with a top that would work for Kate, ASAP. And after a LOT of thinking . . . and several "breakfast" cookies, as I'm calling them, I came up with the redesigned top, featuring spaghetti straps that button on in the back (hard to see in the sketch, but trust me—they're really cool!). It was doable to handsew, and it looked totally AWESOME on Kate! I also made her a matching sling out of the skirt material. Phew! Crisis averted!

And now for another type of Plan B (are you getting today's theme?) . . . My friend-partner Allie Lovallo just texted me that our Etsy pop-up store is now officially SOLD OUT of all merchandise! What??? I can't believe it! Especially since some of the items went to people we didn't even know. (Ha-ha.) It's great news, and I'm so happy that the pop-up shop was a success. But now customers are e-mailing us and asking for more items, and I haven't had time to make any, not without my trusty sewing machine. . . . So what's the Plan B for that??? Feel free to leave suggestions in the comments! My brain is all used up for the day! ☺

In the lunchroom at school on Monday, Zoey raced to her regular table, beating her friends there. She plopped her lunch down and opened up the bag, hoping to find something more exciting than the peanut butter and banana sandwich she'd packed that morning. For some reason, she felt like she wanted something *different* today, but she didn't know what.

Libby was next to appear, and then Kate in her spaghetti-print sling. Priti was still away, and lunch had not been nearly as fun since she'd left.

"So," Zoey asked Kate, "how was the big dinner last night? Did the dress work out okay?"

"I saw the updated sketch on your blog last night!" Libby cut in. "I love the new straps. Kate, do you have a picture on your phone?"

Kate was opening her lunch slowly, a wide, bashful smile creeping across her face. It looked like she had a secret, and it didn't look like it had anything to do with the dress.

"Kate, what is it?" asked Zoey. "Why aren't you talking?"

Kate's cheeks went full-on red. "I won the Most Valuable Player award," she said shyly. "And I had so, so, *so* much fun at the dinner! I didn't even *feel* my elbow the whole night."

"Oh my gosh, Kate!" Zoey was so proud, she felt like she would burst. Of course Kate would win the MVP award! She couldn't believe she hadn't guessed it before. "That's so great!"

"I wish we could have been there," Libby said. "We would have yelled and cheered so loud, we probably would have embarrassed you."

Kate nodded, laughing. "Yeah, you probably would have. But for once I might not have minded."

She pulled her phone out of her backpack and showed the girls a picture her mom had taken of her holding the award after dinner. Kate looked beautiful and happy.

Wow, Kate can really wear clothes! Zoey thought. *She looks like a model in that dress.* She didn't say it out loud, because she knew it might make Kate feel awkward.

Kate must have semi-read her mind, because she turned toward Zoey and said, "Zo, thank you *so* much for fixing the dress. I got compliments on it all night long! Even from our coach! And everyone loves my sling cover, too. Do you think you could . . ." She paused for second, looking uncertain. "Well, I hate to ask you to do more for me because you just helped me so much, but do you think you could make me a few more sling covers to go with some of my school clothes? I don't want to let that ugly hospital one see the light of day ever again!"

Zoey's jaw dropped so low, it very nearly hit her knees. Had Kate been taken over by aliens? Had one successful outfit turned her into a fashionista?

Whatever the reason, Zoey would run with it. "Of *course*," she agreed. "I'll get right on it! They hardly require any sewing at all. And you're right— you can't wear the same one every day. That would be boring."

Libby shook her head a few times. "Kate, I never

thought you'd be concerned about matching. Did you hit your head on the field the other day too?"

All three girls laughed, and Kate replied, "Maybe. Or maybe Zoey's fashion sense is finally rubbing off on me! All I know is that I felt great in that dress last night, and I'm tired of blending in with the wallpaper. Especially the floral wallpaper!"

"All righty, then!" said Zoey. "Get ready, because I might start making you more stuff . . . like maybe even some *skirts* . . ."

Just then, as the girls were having a good time laughing and imagining Kate coming to school in girly outfits every day, Ivy, Shannon, and Bree strolled by on the way to their table. As usual, they had their ears open for anyone else enjoying themselves, so they could chime in and ruin it.

"Nice sling," said Bree in a way that didn't sound very nice at all.

Kate, who didn't have a mean bone in her body, and never knew what to say to sarcastic people, just pressed her lips together and looked down. Zoey and Libby glared at Bree, and Zoey wished Priti were there to tell the girls to buzz off.

"You must have done something pretty clumsy to get that sling," Ivy said. "Did you fall down tying your shoes?" She snickered.

Suddenly, from the table beside theirs, Lorenzo shouted, "Yeah, she's *real* clumsy, Ivy! She sprained her elbow scoring the winning goal at the state championships! You're looking at the team's MVP."

Ivy's face flushed, though probably more from being called out by a boy as cute as Lorenzo than because she'd insulted Kate's athletic ability. She looked like she was about to reply to Lorenzo when Shannon quickly stepped in, touching Ivy's arm to shush her and saying smoothly, "I like your sling, Kate. That fabric is very pretty."

Kate managed to say thank you and tell her that Zoey had made the sling. Shannon met Zoey's eyes, and Zoey could see how much Shannon wished Ivy hadn't been so mean.

Zoey decided to let Shannon off the hook. "I'm going to make her a whole bunch of them," Zoey said nicely, as if the unpleasantness hadn't happened. "To go with all of her outfits until her arm's better."

"That's really nice of you," Shannon said. "C'mon, girls, let's go eat. I'm starving."

Shannon neatly pushed Ivy and Bree along, away from Zoey, Libby, and Kate, and toward their own table. It sure seemed like Shannon was thinking twice about her choice of friends.

"The coast is clear," Libby muttered when the girls were no longer close by. "Whew!"

Zoey looked at Kate, to see if she was okay, but her face was still red, and she was concentrating on her sandwich. Zoey wasn't sure if Kate's embarrassment was from Ivy's nasty comment or because Lorenzo had rushed to her defense so . . . vocally. Zoey had noticed Lorenzo paying more and more attention to Kate lately, and she wondered if Kate had noticed it as well. Kate didn't think of boys as potential *boyfriends*, the way some girls did, so Zoey wasn't sure if she should mention Lorenzo or not. She decided she'd wait a little longer to bring it up, just in case the idea made Kate uncomfortable. After all, Zoey was just getting Kate to be interested in clothes! There was no reason to rush her to be crushing on boys, too.

As the girls were finishing their lunches, Zoey noticed Ms. Austen, the principal, approaching their table. Zoey immediately got nervous that somehow Ms. Austen had heard about the nastiness with Ivy and Bree and was coming to talk to them about it.

But we didn't say anything mean, Zoey reminded herself. *So we can't be in trouble. I don't think . . .*

Ms. Austen, dressed in a chic black shift, with a leopard-print scarf knotted around her neck, and bright green pumps, stopped just beside Zoey.

Zoey saw Libby exchange a nervous look with Kate. Apparently, none of them knew why the principal was singling them out during lunch. But the eyes of nearly every kid in the lunchroom were on their table.

"Hello, girls. Zoey, do you have a second? Can you come with me?" said Ms. Austen cheerily.

Zoey nodded, relieved. Ms. Austen had always been very friendly and supportive of Zoey and her design work, and she didn't sound mad at all. In fact, she sounded excited.

"I have a package for you from *you-know-who* in

my office," she whispered. "It's too heavy to carry here."

A package? A heavy package? Zoey wondered what her secret fashion fan, Fashionsista, who regularly commented on her blog and had sent her several awesome gifts in the past, could have sent now. Zoey was so excited, she jumped up immediately, saying "Be right back!" to Libby and Kate, and following Ms. Austen to the office.

"So how did Kate Mackey's dress work out?" Ms. Austen asked as they turned the corner of the administrative hallway.

Zoey looked at her, surprised. "How'd you know about that?" she asked.

Ms. Austen laughed and flipped her hand at Zoey. "I read your blog, remember? I like to know what my talented students are up to. I really loved the sari you made for Priti, as well."

Zoey felt bowled over by the compliments. Ms. Austen was pretty stylish, and she mixed a lot of great vintage pieces in with her work wardrobe. Not to mention she was the principal, and probably very busy, but still took the time to read Zoey's blog.

"Thank you," said Zoey. "Both dresses turned out really well! I had to learn a lot of new sewing tricks to finish them, though. I spent so much time trying things that didn't work."

"Not so much time that you forgot your homework, I hope," said Ms. Austen, looking serious.

"No," said Zoey quickly. "Well, I did all of my homework, but had trouble fitting in time to study. I got a B+ on Mr. Dunn's test thanks to my study partner, Libby."

"Good." Ms. Austen nodded crisply and opened the door to her office, ushering Zoey inside. "Even fashion designers might need to know when the Mongols ruled China."

Zoey laughed, but stopped suddenly when she saw the huge brown box on Ms. Austen's desk. *That* couldn't be the package for her. It was enormous!

Ms. Austen gestured to the box. "Go on," she said. "I'm dying to know what it is too!"

Still in shock, Zoey accepted a pair of scissors from Ms. Austen and began slicing through the brown packing tape around the box. Carefully, she opened the top, and saw a block of white packing foam. She pried it out, and beneath it was a brand-new, superfancy sewing machine.

"Oh my word!" Ms. Austen exclaimed. "Zoey, this is amazing! Look at all the buttons!"

Zoey's eyes bugged out. It couldn't be, it couldn't be! Very gently, she lifted it out of the foam blocks and set it on Ms. Austen's desk to admire. It was white and shiny and new, with all kinds of features her old machine didn't have, like a needle up-down setting, a locking stitch button, and even a one-hand needle threader!

With this machine, sewing would be so much faster and easier, and her results would be even better!

"Could this really be for me?" she asked, looking at Ms. Austen. "Are you sure this is from Fashionsista?"

"I assumed it was," Ms. Austen replied. "Look for a card."

Peering into the box, Zoey spied an envelope with her name on it, and she quickly pulled it out and opened it. Inside was a note.

Dear Zoey,
    I pulled a few strings (hee-hee) and asked some friends at Speedman Sewing Machines if they would send you a replacement machine since yours is out being repaired. I pointed them to your blog, and after reading about you, they were thrilled to help out! They did ask that you mention this gift and thank them on your blog, for publicity purposes. Sew something fabulous on it!
    Happy sewing!
    Fashionsista

Zoey couldn't believe her good fortune. She was still crushed about her mother's machine, which was currently sitting at a repair shop her father had found, but now she had this amazing new machine to work on. She could probably spend days reading the manual and learning all of its tricks and features. She couldn't even imagine all the wonderful things she could make with it, and all because of her blog, and her readers, and wonderful fans like Fashionsista.

Zoey thought back to just a half hour before, when she'd opened her lunch, and wished for something different. Well, she'd gotten something different all right! She couldn't wait to get the new machine home, to her "fashion studio" in the dining room.

"You must be doing something right, Zoey," Ms. Austen said. "Because you are accumulating some serious fans."

CHAPTER 10

Sew, Sew, Sew FANTASTIC!

You really won't believe this, any of you, but I am sitting here typing this right next to my BRAND-NEW SPEEDMAN SEWING MACHINE! Principal Austen found me at school today and told me I had a package, and it turned out to be from one of the world's BEST fans.

(That's you, FASHIONSISTA! Even though I still don't know who you are. . . .) She arranged for Speedman to send me this completely amazing machine. It does everything. I just started flipping through the manual, and this thing even has an autosensor for making buttonholes. You show it the button, and it makes the hole for you. WHAAAAAT? Everything I make from now on will be covered in buttons. (Hee-hee, I'm kidding about that. Maybe.) So, the only thing to do now is start on some new projects!

Luckily, I'm never short on projects. I'm going to this huge trade show this coming weekend with a REAL fashion buyer, and I'm planning to bring some samples from my accessory line on Etsy. And now that I have this machine, it'll be so much easier to get them done this week! I've even decided to fulfill the extra requests I'd gotten from the Etsy site for made-to-order pieces. I can always use the profit for more fabric, right? After these few requests, though, Allie and I are sticking with our original plan of closing the pop-up shop. Even with my new sewing machine, I have to draw the line somewhere. These last few weeks have been CRAAAAAZY!

I'm sure you're all wondering why I'm blabbing on

about my new machine when I've posted this gorgeous sketch. . . . (At least, I think it's gorgeous.) This is what I'm planning to wear to the trade show on Saturday. I've combined an old denim skirt of my mother's (classic pencil shape), with some other fun pieces from my closet, and a shirt I'm making this week with the same technique Jan used to make her scarves into a belt. I'm thinking of calling it the Tangled Shirt, because of all the fabric that's looped together. What do you think?

I will, of course, be carrying an Accessories from A to Z tote bag from my pop-up shop! I hope to load it up with goodies!

With the trade show to look forward to, and so much sewing and experimenting to do on her new machine, the week flew by. Zoey was enjoying her new Speedman sewing machine so much, she started to feel guilty about it. Her mother's machine continued to sit at the repair shop, and while she missed its familiar, comforting presence, her new machine allowed her to zip through projects faster than she ever had dared dream. She made slings for

Kate, and headbands, belts, and bags to bring to the trade show, and the new shirt. She felt like she could tackle any sewing project that came her way!

Saturday morning, as she was finishing a few of the made-to-order items she'd agreed to do for her final Etsy customers, her phone buzzed. She lunged for it, hoping it was Libby, to discuss the big trade show the following day. Instead, she was thrilled to see it was a text message from Priti, asking her if she could video chat with her in India!

Zoey quickly texted back, **Yes, yes, yes! Just doing some sewing . . . surprise, surprise.**

Zoey logged on to the video chat website and was almost giddy when she saw Priti's face appear on her cell phone's screen, looking shiny and happy against a backdrop of colorful lanterns and well-dressed people dancing.

Zoey realized it had been nearly two weeks since she'd seen her friend. That was way too long as far as she was concerned.

"Priti, I MISS YOU!" Zoey yelled into the phone. "What are you doing?"

Priti grinned. "I'm at the WEDDING! It's

nighttime here in India. I'm wearing your beautiful sari, see?" She held the phone away from her and panned it down, so that Zoey could get a good look at the sari.

"It looks totally awesome," Zoey said. "Are you having the best time? School is not the same without you!"

Priti nodded. "We're having a blast—even my parents are having too much fun to argue. It's been a really good trip for all of us. But, listen, I called you because the funniest thing has happened!"

"Tell me! And hold the phone back a little so I can see the wedding!"

Priti laughed, and turned the phone around so its camera would catch some of the party going on. It looked so beautiful! So much light and color everywhere. Zoey could hear the Indian music, which was loud and joyful, and reminded her of Priti's personality.

"Beautiful!" Zoey exclaimed. "Next time your family goes to India, you're bringing me!"

Priti laughed again, and said, "Okay. It's a deal. Seriously, I called because my cousin's best friend,

Nita, is wearing a sari just like the one you made me! Isn't that funny?"

Zoey was doubtful. A sari *just* like the one she'd made? But Priti's sari was made of a lot of different fabrics sewn together, with ruffles on it and everything. Zoey had designed it to be unique, to be a sari and *not* be a sari at the same time. It seemed very unlikely there would be another one like it.

"Really?" asked Zoey. "Hmm."

"No, *really*," Priti insisted. "Wait a second, I'll find her. . . ."

Zoey watched as the camera's phone bounced around before finally landing on the bride's friend, Nita. There it was—an almost *identical* copy of the sari Zoey had worked so hard to make for Priti.

Zoey was flabbergasted. An identical sari?

"But how?" Zoey managed to sputter. Zoey was nearly certain she'd never seen a design like that before in her life. Although, her life hadn't been a very long one, so maybe there were designs like hers already out there. Still, it seemed unlikely. "How could it be so similar?"

Priti sighed. "Well, Zo, I sent my cousin a link

to the sketch you posted on your blog, because I was *so excited* about you making it, and she likes to sew."

Zoey wondered if Nita might have copied the dress. *Maybe she didn't* intentionally *copy it,* Zoey reasoned. Maybe she saw the sketch, and it stuck in her subconscious or something, and then when she was making herself a sari, it sort of came out looking very similar. That could happen, right? It wasn't *that* big of a deal. It was one dress, one design.

When Zoey didn't speak, Priti continued. "Anyway, Nita thought it was beautiful! She loved it so much, she decided to make it herself!"

Zoey listened but had a hard time keeping a smile on her face. So *that's* why it looked nearly identical—it was. Still, her design . . . her special design! It was incredibly flattering that someone had liked it so much they'd decided to make it themselves, but . . . to copy it exactly?

"And that's not all," Priti went on. "Nita has a clothing shop here in India, and she's getting so many compliments on her sari tonight that she's thinking of selling it in her store! Isn't that *amazing*? You've inspired a real shop owner! You're so talented, Zoey!"

Zoey stared at her phone, watching the beautiful wedding going on behind the image of Priti's familiar face. The moment felt surreal. There Priti was, one of her best friends, halfway around the world, telling her someone in another country was going to copy one of her designs and sell it in a store.

Zoey felt like the wind had been knocked out of her. She was at a loss for words.

"Priti, I . . . I," she started to say. She wasn't sure quite what to say to Priti, who seemed to think this was all good news. "That's *my* design," she finally managed to say. "How can she copy it and put it in her store?"

To Priti's credit, she looked truly confused. "What do you mean, how? Remember when you saw that dress you loved in *Très Chic* that was, like, a million dollars? And you said you loved it and wanted to make one? You did! You made a dress just like it! And you've worn it all over the place. Well, you would have if Buttons hadn't peed on it."

Zoey bit her lip. That was true, she had made a copy of a big designer dress. And there was hardly a difference between it and the real version Libby had worn . . . and had since given to Zoey to keep after hers was ruined.

"But it's different," Zoey tried to explain. "I wasn't making copies to sell to other people. I just made one for myself. You know what I mean?"

Priti nodded, looking crestfallen. She thought she'd been giving Zoey good news. "Yeah, I guess, but since it's all the way over here in India, I thought you'd just be flattered. . . . Wait, hang on."

Priti's face disappeared and the camera pointed directly at the waist of her sari. She heard what sounded like Mrs. Holbrooke talking to Priti, then Priti reappeared.

"Hey, my mom says I need to stop video chatting and hang out with my family. Listen, I'm sorry! I'll call you back as soon as I can!"

The video chat disconnected, and Zoey was left staring at her phone. She looked back at the accessories she'd been working on, intending to pick up where she'd left off before the call. But for some reason she didn't feel like sewing.

Zoey flopped on her bed and grabbed an old stuffed animal she refused to put away in the attic, because sometimes there were days when a girl just needed a stuffed animal to hug. Hers was an elephant, and she squeezed him tight and thought about her conversation with Priti.

She didn't know what to think of what Nita had done, and she felt confused about the whole situation. Was it okay, or wasn't it?

Her phone buzzed again, and reluctantly Zoey grabbed it to see the message. It was Priti, of course, with a long e-mail.

Zoey,

I'm hiding in the bathroom typing this so my mom won't see. I feel TERRIBLE I made you so upset! I honestly thought you'd be so excited. I talked to Nita just now and told her how you felt, and that it was YOUR design, etc., etc. And she said that designs can't be copyrighted, not really, and, anyway, she loves the sari sooooo much that it would be a shame to not make it available, just to a few people here in India.

But she doesn't want to upset you.

I really, really feel terrible, because you are my bestie-bestie and I hate anything that makes you unhappy! I'll be home in just a few days, and I'll fill you in on the whole trip, and maybe, hopefully, I can make this whole mess up to you! Please tell me you feel okay about all this.

Hugs,
Priti

Zoey turned off her phone's screen and rolled over, curling up on her side. She didn't feel okay. In fact, she felt sort of sick over the idea of someone else making and selling her very special design. She wrote a quick e-mail back to Priti saying that she wasn't sure how she felt about it yet, but wishing her a great rest of the trip.

Zoey thought and thought about it. Was this what the "real world" of fashion design was all about? She didn't think so. All her experiences with it so far had been amazing, and she was learning more and loving it more every single day. Had Daphne Shaw ever had this happen to her?

She knew, without a doubt, that being a designer was her life's dream. And most of that dream was incredible. So if this was part of it, well, as her dad said, she'd have to roll with the punches.

CHAPTER 11

Reflections: Good, Bad, and In-Between

My dad always, always, ALWAYS tells me that in life, you have to take the good with the bad. And that's certainly been true for me this week!

I'll start with the GOOD, because I'm an optimistic person. ☺ My new Speedman sewing machine is the most fantastic sewing machine on the planet! Maybe the solar system. Do you think they have sewing machines on other planets? I couldn't have dreamed up such a great machine! It's inspired me to try to make this outfit I've been thinking about—see my sketch—made with a mirror-image patterned fabric. These fabrics are kind of pricey, and tricky to sew with because you have to make sure it's all lined up perfectly, and smooth as silk, but I'm ready for a challenge!

And now for the BAD. ☹ (C'mon, I told you it was coming!) It seems that someone really liked one of my designs I posted on this blog (which is flattering), and not only made a copy of the dress for herself, but is planning to produce the dress and SELL it in her store in India (which is not flattering . . .). That's why I've been thinking about duplicates and mirror images, so at least I got a fun idea out of it.

But I'm really confused about this. Are people allowed to do that? To take someone else's design and knowingly copy it and reproduce it? I know about knockoffs, but I'm not exactly a big, established designer who's so amazing that they inspire knockoffs!

A little while ago I made a copy of a dress I loved

but couldn't afford. Now that I know what it feels like to be copied, I feel like I should apologize to that designer. But I didn't try to sell it. Somehow, that feels different.

Anyway, I don't know all the rules of fashion and copyrighting designs and whatnot yet, so if any of my wise readers have some advice to give me, I'm all ears!

The morning of the trade show, Zoey was nervous. Well, nervous-excited. She'd never been to an event like this before, not to mention she'd be spending time with Libby's aunt, who was a real industry professional and knew exactly what kind of designs were likely to sell in stores. It would truly be an amazing day, or at least she hoped it would!

Which is why I need an amazing outfit, Zoey told herself, looking in the mirror and trying to figure out what was missing. She was wearing the Tangled top, cheetah-print leggings, her mom's skirt, and a pair of lace-up sandals that tied above the ankle. Her hair was up in a tight ballerina bun. But *something* was missing!

She grabbed a clutch from her tote bag full of samples to bring to the trade show. The clutch looked perfect with her outfit, but the thought of having to hold it in her hand all day didn't sound so perfect.

That's it! Zoey thought. She grabbed one of the belts she'd made and looped it through the flap of the clutch to make an impromptu cross-body bag.

"Cool!" Zoey said to her reflection in the mirror.

Just then, the doorbell rang, and Zoey grabbed her lucky lip gloss and her tote bag, and ran down the stairs. She could hardly wait.

Marcus beat her to the door. Zoey ran up behind him, just as he was opening it. Allie stood on the front steps, with Libby and her aunt.

"Oh, wow, hi," Marcus said, sounding slightly flustered.

Zoey wondered if he'd been expecting someone else. She'd *told* him they were all coming this morning to take her to the show.

"Marcus, you remember . . . ," she started to say.

"Allie, yeah, hi," he said quickly.

"Hi, Marcus," Allie replied, looking slightly pink.

Allie had dressed for the trade show as well, and she looked very chic in a shirtdress with a wide belt, and a pair of tall boots.

Zoey realized Priti had been right—Marcus did like Allie. And why shouldn't he? They were about the same age. Why should she care if her brother and her friend liked each other? She decided she would help him out. After all, he had helped her out *hugely* lately with chores and dishes and Etsy stuff. And he even drove her around sometimes. Zoey resolved to drop a few comments to Allie that day about how great her brother is, and what a good drummer and a nice guy, and see how she reacted. Maybe she would have a career as a matchmaker *and* a designer!

The thought almost made her laugh, but then Libby stepped forward to introduce Zoey to her aunt.

"This is Zoey," Libby said excitedly, "my famous designer friend. Zo, this is my aunt, Alexandra Van Langen."

Zoey turned a bright tomato red at the word "famous," because she was anything but.

"It's nice to meet you, Ms. Van Langen," Zoey said, trying to sound mature.

"It's so nice to meet *you*," said Libby's aunt. "And, please, just call me Aunt Lexie. Libby does. Now, Zoey, I've been really impressed with your blog, and your entry from the recent sewing contest, *and* your pop-up shop on Etsy. Not to mention you've been such a wonderful friend to Libby!"

Zoey felt like she might explode from all the praise. Lexie Van Langen thought *she* was impressive?

"Thank you," Zoey said graciously. "But it's really such an honor to meet you! I love your store, and I think your job must be one of the most fun jobs on the planet!"

Aunt Lexie laughed. "Well," she said, leaning in conspiratorially, "I'll tell you a secret. It is! I get to see all the best and newest fashions and accessories, and pick which ones we sell at H. Cashin's. It's like shopping all day, every day. And today is particularly fun, not only because I have you, Libby, and Allie as my companions, but because this particular trade show is known for featuring up-and-coming new designers. We're going to see some really edgy and innovative things today!"

Zoey couldn't help bouncing on her feet, she was so excited to get going. She felt like a sprinter at the starting line.

"Well, bye, Marcus," Zoey said, starting to close the door.

"Have fun, All—" He turned red. "I—I mean, see you later, alligator! Have fun . . . everyone."

He is acting so weird, Zoey thought before waving good-bye.

"You too!" Allie said as Zoey started to close the door behind them.

They followed Lexie to her car. Once they were all settled inside, Zoey noticed Aunt Lexie had the clutch Zoey had made from the Etsy site resting on the front seat. She was actually carrying it that day!

Zoey wanted to swoon. She looked over at Allie, who was sharing the backseat with her, and mouthed, *Isn't this amazing?*

Allie nodded and then reached across the seat to squeeze Zoey's hand. *Amazing,* she mouthed back.

The ride to the trade show was about as fascinating as a ride could be. Zoey and Allie took turns asking Aunt Lexie questions about her job and learned more about the world of a department store buyer. Everything Lexie said captivated Zoey. It was like a behind-the-scenes peek every designer needed to understand why a buyer would, or would not, choose to carry their item in a store.

They pulled into the parking lot at the convention center, where the trade show was being held. After a short walk they arrived at the wide double-door entrance to the main room. Aunt Lexie checked in with two women at a long table, who handed her several badges, each on a lanyard, for them to wear inside. Zoey slipped hers over her head, feeling very important.

When they stepped through the doors, Zoey couldn't help from grabbing Libby's hand. They looked at each other. It was accessories heaven! Row after row of booths, each one displaying beautiful, unique crafts and accessories.

"This is too amazing. I feel like I'm dreaming," Zoey whispered.

"Me too!" said Libby, giggling.

Even Allie, normally cool and collected, looked overwhelmed by where to begin. There was almost *too* much to see.

Aunt Lexie noticed all three girls were standing frozen, rooted to the spot and unsure how to even start to enjoy all the amazing merchandise.

"It feels overwhelming, right?" Lexie said. "It's always like this. I find it helps to have a game. Why don't you girls go up and down the aisles, and from each row you have to pick your *one* favorite item? Just for fun—because the things here, the samples, aren't for sale. Okay?"

"Okay!" the girls all agreed, glad to have something to help them focus. They were like little kids in a candy store.

The girls began moving up and down the aisles, stopping at each booth, carefully picking and choosing their favorites and enjoying the variety of items at the show. All the designers were superfriendly and happy to answer questions from the girls, even though they knew the girls weren't buyers, of course.

Libby's aunt walked around with them for a while, then dropped them at the H. Cashin's booth, so Zoey and Allie could show some of Lexie's coworkers the accessories they'd made.

Zoey was so excited, she let Allie go first, so she could have a minute to collect herself and talk slowly. She knew it was important to make a good impression. When she finally did show them her things, she was surprised by how gracious and kind they all were. Many of them said they'd heard of Zoey and Allie and had checked out their pop-up shop. A few of them even bought samples from the girls to give to their kids and nieces.

Zoey felt like she might be having one of the best days of her life. Could it get any better than this?

They stayed at the show for hours, until Zoey almost felt like she couldn't walk another step, and even her eyes felt heavy from looking at so many beautiful things.

When Aunt Lexie suggested they go, Zoey agreed. Her brain was bursting, trying to remember every single thing she'd seen, and she felt the urge to go home and sketch immediately. She had so many new ideas! So many new things she wanted to try.

Back at the car, as everyone was putting on their seat belts, Aunt Lexie held up her tote bag from the trade show.

"Do you know what's in here?" she asked.

The girls shook their heads, confused.

Aunt Lexie laughed, and then opened the bag, presenting each girl with one of the "favorite" accessories they'd picked during their game. Zoey and the other girls were thrilled! Lexie had gone back and convinced the vendors to give them as gifts to the girls as mementos of their wonderful day. She gave a ruffled messenger bag to Libby, a fluorescent green studded belt to Allie, and a cuff bracelet with intricate silver work to Zoey. Zoey slipped it on and sighed, feeling so happy from the events of the day.

Then the dark, nagging thing that had been bothering her ever since her video chat with Priti reared its ugly head. No matter how hard she tried, Zoey just couldn't get Nita's copied dress out of her head. She decided she would ask Aunt Lexie about it. After all, she'd probably know the answer, or at least be able to offer some advice.

She quickly explained the situation to Lexie, with Libby helpfully filling in the cracks.

"So is that allowed?" Zoey asked. "You know, to produce and sell my design that she got from the sketch on my blog?"

"Well," said Aunt Lexie. "I'm afraid you're not going to like my answer. But, yes, it is 'allowed,' as you say. Although, in my opinion, not in very good taste. It's just too hard to copyright clothing design to make it possible to police something like that."

Zoey nodded, relieved at least to have a real answer from someone. If it was legal, and there was nothing she could do about it, well, then, there was really not much point to being upset about it, she supposed. She'd just have to move on.

"However," Aunt Lexie went on, "think about it this way. If someone is so impressed with your designs that they want to produce and carry them in a shop, it's because they *know* they'll be able to sell them. So that means there's a market for your work! Maybe it's time for you to sell some of your clothes online, now that you've gotten your feet wet with your accessories pop-up shop and Doggie Duds. What do you think?"

"That's a great idea!" Libby chimed in right away. "Oh, do it, Zoey!"

Allie nodded. "I totally agree. You sold out all of your accessories so fast! You could start the clothing line small, with just a few items, and see how it goes."

Zoey shook her head in disbelief. She didn't know what to think. Just a short time ago she was a complete sewing novice, just trying to make a simple beach cover-up. And now someone, a real buyer at a big department store, was telling her she should start selling her clothes online?

"This has been the most amazing day *ever*," Zoey announced, grinning at everyone. "I think I'm going to go for it."

CHAPTER 12

Sew Zoey ... the Store!

I can't believe I'm doing this, but guess what???
I've decided to put up my own Sew Zoey shop on Etsy
(with my dad's help, of course)! And not a pop-up this
time—a real shop. For now, the pieces will be one-of-
a-kind, with just a few starter pieces available at the

moment, but I'll be taking specials orders based on people's sizes. I might even include a few of the Doggie Duds outfits for people who didn't get to take part in the campaign. After all, those outfits were REALLY fun to make, and those dogs have been some of my happiest customers! ☺

I want to also say a big THANK YOU to Aunt Lexie for taking me to the trade show over the weekend, which really opened my eyes to all the great stuff out there, and for encouraging me to try my own shop!

I can't wait to tell my dad. . . . I think he thought he might be getting the dining room back soon. . . . Hee-hee. But it looks like it'll be Sew Zoey headquarters for quite a while. In fact, my "headquarters" will have TWO machines in it! The repair shop finally called and said they were able to fix my mom's machine. I can't WAIT to have it back! I sort of miss its lack of fancy buttons. ☺ I'll still use my Speedman machine for tricky projects, of course . . . or when I want to sew something super-duper ultra fast! For sentimental reasons, I'll probably keep using my mom's for daily sewing: It's kind of like having her here. Thanks again, Speedman Sewing Machines, for saving me from sewing doom and giving me this amazing gift.

Here's a sketch of an outfit I'm thinking of putting in my shop. (I like the sound of that already. . . .) The pants are in a pink fabric I found at A Stitch in Time. Don't they look fun? I can't wait to wear them!

To celebrate Priti's return from India that week, Zoey invited her, Kate, and Libby over for a pizza-and-hang-out night. It had been way too long since the four of them had had a chance to get together outside of school.

Everyone showed up after school on Friday, ready for some serious girlfriend time. Zoey had made mini pizza bagels as snacks ahead of time, and she was pulling a batch out of the toaster oven as everyone started arriving.

Kate came in first, wearing one of the sporty slings Zoey had made for her. She plopped herself down at the kitchen counter and grabbed a pizza bagel.

"When do you get the sling off?" Zoey asked, watching as Kate carefully blew on the hot toppings before popping the bagel into her mouth.

"Next week!" Kate answered. "It's feeling a lot better, actually. I've definitely missed playing sports the past few weeks, but whenever I get too bummed, I just look at my MVP trophy, and I feel like it was worth it."

"It *was* worth it," Zoey agreed. "You scored the winning goal! And you'll be playing again really soon."

"Exactly," said Kate. "And for once I've actually had some time to hang out with friends! A bunch of the girls from my soccer team, and, um, some boys, are all going to the movies tomorrow night."

Kate blushed, and Zoey's eyes went wide. "Boys? Which ones?"

Kate nodded. "Um, yeah. Like, you know, Lorenzo and his friends. It's just a big group of us going to the movies."

Kate's words made it sound like nothing, but her face told a different story. This time, Zoey felt certain Kate had noticed Lorenzo was a boy and quite possibly even liked him.

"Well, I think it's cool you're all going out," Zoey

said. "If you want, I could help you pick out an outfit to wear."

Kate smiled and looked relieved Zoey hadn't asked for more details. "That'd be great, thanks."

"And Lorenzo's pretty nice," Zoey continued as Kate's cheeks turned red, "but I've been thinking he and I should just be friends, you know?"

"Really?" Kate asked quietly. Then her eyes lit up. "Well, I guess we better find you a new crush."

The girls were still laughing when there was a knock at the door. Priti and Libby came in together, already talking a mile a minute.

"I've brought PICTURES!" Priti announced, seating herself beside Kate and holding up her phone. "Pictures of the wedding in India! And of the sacred cows in India. And so much. I can't wait to show you guys."

"I can't wait to see them!" Libby exclaimed. Then she sniffed the air. "Is that pizza I smell? Yum!"

"Pizza *bagels*," Zoey said as she transferred the bagels from the toaster oven cookie sheet to a plate, and then put them in front of the girls. She loved having all her friends over, with absolutely nothing for them to do but talk and catch up. Next to sewing, it was her favorite thing in the world.

Libby nudged Zoey's elbow. "Guess what? My aunt's coworkers keep talking about you and Allie and how talented you are and how they can't wait to buy things on your Sew Zoey shop on Etsy. So I hope you've gotten started!"

Zoey smiled shyly, looking both pleased and excited by the idea that she might already have her first customers. "Well, actually, Dad thought it was a great idea, so we already launched it," she admitted, "but with just a few items so far. I plan to add more this weekend. Tonight is my night off!"

"Well, we're honored to have you all to ourselves for the night," said Priti. "Or mostly to ourselves. Where are Marcus and your dad?"

Zoey giggled. She couldn't help it. Every time she thought about where Marcus was, it made her giggle. "*Marcus* won't be here, because he's out on a date . . . with Allie!"

Libby and Kate looked up, surprised. But Priti just nodded her head. "That's right," she said. "Sounded like puppy love."

"Tell us everything!" Libby said.

"Well, he'd been asking me a lot about her. And then last weekend, when she came by, I noticed how they looked at each other. So I gave him a nudge and told him to call her. So he did, and I think they talked like *every* night this week. And then he asked her out for a movie tonight, and she said yes!"

"That's great," said Kate. "Marcus is such a nice guy."

"He is," Zoey agreed. "And a nice brother, too. And, well, you know I adore Allie."

"Speaking of nice guys," said Priti. "Did you ever clear things up with Gabe?"

Zoey colored slightly. She had forgotten she had even mentioned to her friends that Gabe had offered to help her study. "There isn't anything to clear *up*, really. He was just so nice to want to help. So I'm making him a Doggie Duds outfit for his schnauzer, Mr. Paws. I'm going to finish it this weekend and give it to him on Monday. That's a nice thing to do, right?"

Libby nodded vigorously. "Yes, definitely. Our

dog loves his. And then Gabe will know you really do like him as a friend."

"Exactly," Zoey agreed.

"Is it picture time yet?" Priti asked. "Because I'm dying to show you guys all the stuff we did on our trip. . . ."

"Okay, okay, we're ready!" Kate declared. "But bring the pizza bagels."

The girls moved to the family room, where they could all jam together on the couch to look at Priti's slideshow. Surrounded by her best friends, Zoey felt content. She had an Etsy shop all her own, two working sewing machines, and three best friends she knew she could count on. Life didn't get much better!

After everyone's parents had come to pick them up, Zoey stood in the kitchen, cleaning up the dishes. Her dad had gone to sleep early, and Marcus still wasn't back from his date with Allie. Zoey's phone buzzed, and she reached for it, assuming it was Marcus checking in with her and their dad.

Instead, it was an e-mail from her new Sew Zoey

shop, alerting her that she had her first order. Zoey clicked through to read the details. *It's probably Aunt Lulu again,* she thought as she scrolled through the text.

But the name on the order wasn't Lulu this time. It was Daphne Shaw! Daphne was Zoey's dream designer—her idol, really. And she wanted to buy a shirt from Zoey!

Zoey couldn't believe it. She couldn't believe she was standing in her kitchen, loading the dishwasher and getting an order from Daphne Shaw, all at the same time. It was just too awesome.

When she scrolled down farther, she saw there was a message included. It read:

Hi, Zoey!

Love your new Etsy shop! I'm so glad you opened it. I was serious about inviting you up to New York to visit my design studio. Let's make a plan! Talk to your dad and let me know when you can come. I can't wait to meet you.

All the best,
Daphne Shaw

Zoey dropped the spatula onto the kitchen floor. Daphne Shaw was following up with *her* to make sure she came to New York to hang out with her at her studio?

What on earth would she *wear*?

Want to keep reading?
Knot to worry!
Turn the page for a
sneak peek at the next book
in the Sew Zoey series:

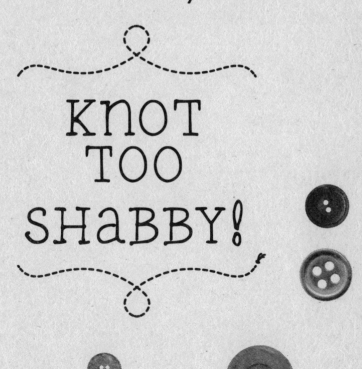

KNOT
TOO
SHABBY!

Fun in the Sun!

I can't believe how fast this school year has flown by! Summer vacation is just around the corner, and so far I'm planning on spending as much time as possible at Camp Lulu and the beach. It seems like only yesterday I got the text message from Priti, just before school started, telling me that our new principal, Ms. Austen, ended the uniform policy and made my dreams come true. I still get excited, just thinking about it. ☺ Yay, Ms. Austen!

But so much has happened since then. I started my Sew Zoey blog, thinking only my family and a few friends would read it, or maybe no one at all. But it really took off, and through my blog I've "met" all of you awesometastic readers and learned so much from you. Sew Zoey has led to things I wouldn't have imagined in my wildest dreams, like being picked for a *Très Chic* website feature and starting online shops for dog (and human) clothes!

I won't pretend it's *all* been fun and games. Sometimes it's been a teensy bit overwhelming. And that, my friends, is the understatement of the century. But I wouldn't trade this year for *anything*. I can't wait to see what new adventures this summer will bring! I just hope it involves plenty of fun in the sun at the beach, which happened to have inspired this sketch.

"This is my favorite day of the school year," Kate Mackey said as she and Zoey Webber waited for Ms. Brown, their language arts teacher, to pass out their yearbooks. "I love the first time we get to look through the yearbook."

Zoey loved getting her yearbook too, but she wasn't sure she'd go as far as saying it was her *favorite* day of the school year.

"I'm always afraid that there won't be any pictures of me or that there will be a picture of me but an awful one," Zoey said.

"You worry too much, Zo," Kate said. "I bet there will be a picture of you, and you'll look fab in it."

Ms. Brown handed Kate her book and checked off her name against her list.

"And here you go, Zoey," she said, handing Zoey hers. "Planning on launching any exciting new businesses this summer?"

"No," Zoey said. "I need a rest from all ones I started during the school year!"

"Keep at it," encouraged Ms. Brown. "I think it's wonderful you're following your passion."

"I will," Zoey said. "But *after* I spend some time at the pool!"

They didn't have much time to look through their yearbooks before Ms. Brown started class— only as long as it took her to give out the rest of the books to the students.

"Look, Zo! There's a great picture of you, me, Priti, and Libby on the dance floor," Kate said. "And we're all wearing the tiaras you made us."

"You mean from the Sadie Hawkins dance?" Zoey asked.

"Yeah—look!"

It was a great picture. They'd all worried so much about asking a boy to the dance, but in the end they'd had the best time going together as a group—four besties being one another's "dates."

It wasn't until lunchtime that Zoey and her friends had the time to really check out the yearbook.

"Oh my gosh, Zoey. Did you see you were voted Best Dressed?" Libby Flynn exclaimed.

"No way! What page? Show me!" Zoey shrieked.

Libby passed her yearbook to Zoey, opened to the awards section. Sure enough, there were several pictures of Zoey wearing her own homemade fashion creations.

"I can't believe it!" Zoey said.

"Why not?" Priti Holbrooke asked. "You always wear cool clothes!"

"I don't know," Zoey said. "I guess because . . . well, because it means that not everyone feels the same way about my outfits as Ivy Wallace does."

"Of course they don't!" Kate said. "Look how many people read your blog."

"And you were asked to be a guest judge on Fashion Showdown!" Priti reminded her. "That doesn't happen to just anyone. Especially someone who doesn't have fashion sense."

"Ivy Wallace is just jealous," Libby said. "I bet that's why she always says mean things."

"Still, it's nice to know everyone else thinks I'm well-dressed," Zoey said, flipping through the pages of her yearbook. "Hey, look! Priti, you've been voted Most Entertaining!"

"Entertaining? *Moi?* Really?" Priti said, waving her hands in a dramatic gesture. "Let me peruse your yearbook!"

Zoey passed Priti her yearbook so she could see the picture of herself wearing a glittery headband, with jazz hands and a big smile.

"Why, yes, I guess I am the Most Entertaining!" she said. "But where is my Oscar statuette?"

"It's probably still getting engraved." Zoey played along.

Priti giggled.

"Kate, you've been voted Most Likely to Win Olympic Gold!" Libby said, still flipping through the yearbook pages. There were several pictures of Kate—playing soccer and on the swim team.

Kate blushed as she looked at the pictures. "I don't know why. There are lots of good athletes—"

"C'mon, girl—own it!" Priti said.

"You deserve it," Zoey said. "Mapleton Prep wouldn't have done nearly as well in soccer or swimming without you."

"I guess," Kate said. "But—"

"No buts!" Libby said.

"Own it!" Zoey said.

"Okay, okay, I own it," Kate said.

"Say 'I am the bomb,'" Priti instructed.

"Do I have to?" Kate sighed.

"Yes," Libby said.

Zoey agreed with Priti too. Kate sighed.

"Oooookay. I'mthebomb. Satisfied?" Kate said.

"It's a start, but next time, say it like you really mean it," Priti said.

"What about you, Libby?" Kate asked, trying desperately to change the subject from herself. "Did you get an award?"

They all flipped through the awards pages. Sadly, Libby hadn't been voted "best" anything.

"I don't mind," Libby said, "really. Besides, I'm still pretty new here. There's time for me to be best at something."

"Wait, look," Zoey exclaimed. "There's a big picture of you at the fashion show!"

"Ooh, and I'm modeling the dress you made!" Libby said. "Which is still my favorite dress ever, by the way. Well, next to the Libby dress."

"My favorite picture in the whole yearbook is the one of all four of us together," Kate said, turning to the picture of the four girls at the dance.

"Yes!" Priti exclaimed. "I love that one. That was such a fun night."

"That's my favorite, too," Libby said.

"Mine too," Zoey said. "You guys definitely get my vote for Best Besties!"

That night before dinner, Zoey's dad said he had some good news for Zoey.

Zoey was always up for good news.

"I spoke to Erica Hill today," her father said, "and we talked about setting a date for the visit."

Zoey was confused.

"Who is Erica Hill, and what visit?" she asked.

Mr. Webber grinned. "Erica Hill is the assistant to a fashion designer by the name of Daphne Shaw. I think you might have heard of her."

"What? We're going to visit Daphne's studio? Yippeeeee!" Zoey shrieked. "It's really happening?"

"Huh? I can't hear you. Um . . . I think you just

broke my eardrums," Marcus, Zoey's older brother, complained.

"Sorry, Marcus," Zoey said. "But . . . it's Daphne Shaw!!! Can you blame me for being excited? When are we going, Dad? When?"

"The Friday after school gets out," Dad explained. "Erica and I actually talked about the visit a while back, but we agreed it would make more sense to wait till the summer, when you were out of school and the studio wasn't so busy. Daphne wanted to make sure she has time to show you around personally and take you out to lunch."

Zoey hugged her dad and then started dancing around the kitchen in excitement, singing a little victory song. "I'm going to New Yo-orrrk, to meet Daphne Sha-awww!" she sang. "She's taking me to lu-unnnch!"

"I'm going to go cray-zee if Zo-eeey doesn't stop sing-innng" Marcus sang in a groaning parody of his sister. "Dad, please. Make. It. Sto-oppp!"

"Actually, I was wondering, Zoey . . ." Her dad hesitated, and Zoey stopped dancing and singing because he sounded serious. "Well, I can drive you to New York and take you to the studio. . . . It's just, well, you know what my fashion sense is like. On a scale of one to ten, it's a negative five."

"Negative five is being way too hard on yourself, Dad. I'd have said you were at least a three. I'd even go as high as a four or a five when you aren't wearing sweats," Zoey joked.

"Well, since we're going to the fashion district, to meet a top designer who is your inspiration, the last thing I want to do is embarrass you by showing up in some fuddy-duddy outfit. So what do you say we hit the mall tonight, and you can help me pick out a more fashion forward outfit?"

"Yes! I'd be happy to be your fashion adviser," Zoey said, giving her father another hug. It was really kind of cute when he admitted he was prone to making fashion faux pas. She couldn't wait to take him shopping!

Later that night, Marcus and his band were practicing in the basement. Mr. Webber ordered them pizza for dinner so that he and Zoey could get an early start at the mall.

"You can have your pick of the food court," Dad said as they pulled out of the garage.

"After we find you an outfit," Zoey corrected. "Fashion comes first!"

"I should have known." Dad sighed. "Duds before grub."

Rain pelted down on the roof of the car so hard that Zoey almost had to shout to be heard.

"It better not be like this when school gets out," Zoey complained. "My friends and I have important poolside plans, and the pool and the pouring rain don't mix."

"Don't worry, Zo," her dad said. "It's probably just a passing downpour."

Sure enough, by the time they got to the mall, the rain had lightened to a drizzle and the sun was trying to peek its way through the clouds on the horizon.

"Look, Dad, a rainbow!" Zoey exclaimed.

"Even better, a double rainbow," her dad said. "That's extra good luck."

"If I have much more good luck, I might explode from excitement," Zoey said. . . .

CHLOE TAYLOR

learned to sew when she was a little girl. She loved watching her grandmother Louise turn a scrap of blue fabric into a simple-but-fabulous dress, nightgown, or even a bathing suit in an instant. It was magical! Now that she's grown up, she still loves fashion: it's like art that you can wear. This is her first middle grade series. She lives, writes, and window-shops in New York City.

NANCY ZHANG

is an illustrator and an art and fashion lover with a passion for all beautiful things. She has published her work in the art books *L'Oiseau Rouge* and *Street Impressions* and in various fashion magazines and on websites. Visit her at her blog: www.xiaoxizhang.com. She currently lives in Berlin, Germany.

Great stories are like great accessories:
You can never have too many! Collect all
the books in the Sew Zoey series:

Ready to Wear

On Pins and Needles

Lights, Camera, Fashion!

Stitches and
Stones

Cute as a Button

A Tangled Thread

Knot Too Shabby!